IT BEGAN IN
FIRE . . .

. . . the fire that burned innocent Susannah
Goode at the stake. But the Goodes had their
revenge. They cursed the Fiers forever.

The curse brought death and destruction to
generations of Fiers—until Simon came along.

Simon thinks he's beaten the curse. He's
changed his family name to Fear. He has the
powerful amulet his ancestors wore. He's gone to
New Orleans to start a new life. Nothing's going
to stop him.

That's what Simon thinks.

No one escapes from the curse.

It began in fire . . . and now it ends with The
Burning.

THE FEAR STREET® SAGA ③
R·L·STINE

The Burning

AN ARCHWAY PAPERBACK
Published by POCKET BOOKS
New York London Toronto Sydney Singapore

This book is a work of fiction. Names, characters, places and
incidents are products of the author's imagination or are used
fictitiously. Any resemblance to actual events or locales or persons,
living or dead, is entirely coincidental.

AN ARCHWAY PAPERBACK *Original*

An Archway Paperback published by
POCKET BOOKS, a division of Simon & Schuster, Inc.
1230 Avenue of the Americas, New York, NY 10020

ISBN: 0-671-86833-0

First Archway Paperback printing October 1993

10   9   8   7

AN ARCHWAY PAPERBACK and colophon are
registered trademarks of Simon & Schuster, Inc.

Cover art by Bill Schmidt

Printed in the U.S.A.

IL 7+

THE FIER FAMILY TREE

Constance ═ Matthew (brothers) Benjamin ═ Margaret
(b. 1675) │ (b. 1660)   (b. 1653) │ (b. 1657)

Mary   Rebecca ═ Edward
(b. 1693)   (b. 1686) │ (b. 1674)

Jane ═ Ezra
(b. 1707) │ (b. 1704)

Delilah ═ Jonathan   Abigail   Rachel
(b. 1727) (b. 1725)   (b. 1729)   (b. 1734)

(100-Year Break)

Samuel ═ Katherine
(b. 1802) (b. 1806)

Angelica ═ Simon (Fear)   Kate   Elizabeth
(b. 1828) (b. 1825)   (b. 1826) (b. 1827)

Julia   Hannah   Brandon
(b. 1848) (b. 1849)   (b. 1854)

Robert ═ Rose   Joseph ═ Amelia
(b. 1851) │ (b. 1859) (b. 1860) │ (b. 1864)

Sarah ═ Thomas   Nora ═ Daniel
(b. 1878) (b. 1876)   (b. 1884) (b. 1882)

Village of Shadyside
1900

The candle flickered low. Candle wax puddled on the narrow wooden tabletop.

Nora Goode set down her pen and stretched. Her shoulders ached. She rubbed her tired eyes.

Shadows cast by the single candle danced around the small room. Nora raised her eyes to the small window. Pale gray light seeped in between the bars.

The first light of morning, Nora thought. She felt a stab of panic in her chest.

The first light of morning, and I still have so much to write.

She flexed her aching fingers, then picked up the pen. "I must finish my story before they come for me," she murmured.

The story of the two families—the Fears and the

1

Goodes. The story of the evil curse that followed them through time.

So much to tell.

She had been writing all night, but she knew she had to continue. Nora swept her dark hair back over her shoulders. Then gave a start.

What was that darting shadow against the wall?

Nora turned to see a scrawny rat scamper across the bare floorboards toward her feet.

Ignore it, she told herself. Do not be distracted, Nora. This story is too important.

It must be told. It must be written.

If I do not finish the story of the Fears, no one will know how to stop the evil. Then the horrors will continue forever.

Nora hunched over the table and started to write again. I must now tell the story of Simon Fear, she decided.

To try to avoid the family curse, Simon changed his name from Fier to Fear. As a young man of twenty-one, he moved to New Orleans to seek his fortune.

Nora shook her head bitterly. Did Simon really believe he could leave two hundred years of evil behind him?

Ignoring the scratching of the rat, ignoring the sputtering of the dying candle, Nora dipped her pen in the inkwell and continued to write. . . .

PART ONE

New Orleans, Louisiana
1845

Chapter
1

———————

Simon Fear stopped in front of the white picket fence that stretched the length of the sprawling white mansion. Through the enormous front window he could see the partygoers in fancy dress.

It was brighter than day inside the ballroom. The light from the window swept over the front lawn. Horse-drawn carriages waited in line by the entrance to let off their passengers. A row of servants in uniform stood ready to assist them.

Simon hesitated. He pulled at the cuffs of his jacket. The sleeves were too short. His shirt cuffs were frayed. He had no ruffles on his shirtfront.

These are the wealthiest society people in New Orleans, he told himself, watching a woman in a full, three-tiered pink ball gown enter the white-columned mansion. Do I really have the nerve to enter this party without an invitation?

The answer, of course, was *yes*.

Before dressing for the party, Simon had made a mental list of his assets:

I am good-looking.

I can be very charming and witty if I desire to be.

I am as smart as anyone in New Orleans.

I am determined to do anything it takes to be a success.

Taking a deep breath, Simon straightened his black cape with the purple satin lining and strode up to the gate, his eyes on the entrance.

I am sure that Mr. Henry Pierce and his charming daughter, Angelica, would have invited me to their debutante ball if they had known me, Simon told himself.

Well, tonight I will give them a chance to get to know me.

And I will take this opportunity to introduce myself to as many wealthy young ladies as I can. After tonight I will not have to sneak into parties. The invitations will pour in.

Simon stopped at the gate. From inside the open double doors he could hear laughter, the clink of glasses, and the soft music of a string quartet.

These sounds were being repeated all over the town. It was Mardi Gras, and all of New Orleans was celebrating with masked balls, debutante parties, and wild, noisy street parades.

The fancy-dress ball Henry Pierce was throwing for his daughter, Angelica, was the most exclusive party of them all, which was why Simon had selected it.

But now, gazing at the line of servants that blocked his way to the entrance, Simon began to lose confidence.

Can I really get past them? he wondered, pulling nervously at his jacket cuffs. Have I come this far only to be turned away?

No. I cannot deprive the beautiful and wealthy young women of my company.

Without any further hesitation Simon swept his cape behind him and moved through the gate and up the wide stairs.

"I beg your pardon, sir." A white-haired servant wearing a tailcoat over old-fashioned knee breeches and a red satin waistcoat stepped forward, his hand outstretched. "May I see your invitation?"

"My invitation?" Simon smiled at the servant, his dark eyes flashing in the bright gaslight. "Why, yes, of course," he said, stalling for time.

Reaching into his coat pocket, Simon dipped his head and deliberately caused his black top hat to fall off. The hat bounced onto the wide porch.

Pretending to reach for it, Simon kicked it toward the door.

"Allow me to get that for you, sir," the servant said, moving quickly toward the hat.

But Simon was quicker. He scooped up the hat by its brim, then threw his arm around the shoulders of a smartly dressed gentleman just entering the house.

"Why, George, old fellow! How good to see you

7

again!" Simon declared loudly, keeping his arm around the man's shoulders and entering the house with him.

"Do I *know* you?" the startled man cried.

"So sorry. My mistake," Simon replied with a curt bow.

The servant stepped into the doorway to search for Simon. But he had already lost himself in the crowd.

He was breathing hard, excited by his daring entrance. His smile remained confident as he handed his cape and hat to a servant and moved into the ballroom.

Crystal chandeliers hung low from the ceiling, sending a blaze of yellow gaslight over the crowded room. The vast floor was an intricate pattern of dark and light inlaid wood. The walls were covered in brocade.

Simon studied the young women, such beautiful young women, with sausage curls framing the sides of their glowing faces. Their long hooped ball gowns swept across the shiny floor. Their voices chimed brightly. Their laughter tinkled like the clink of champagne glasses.

The men strutted about in their dark tailcoats and taper-legged trousers. Simon scoffed at their flowing white cravats and ruffled white shirts, scoffed and envied them at the same time.

It takes more than a ruffled shirt to make a gentleman, he reminded himself.

I am as much a gentleman as any of these peacocks. And some day I will have a wardrobe full of ruffled shirts, shirts to put all of these dandies to shame.

In the far corner a string quartet played Haydn. Simon started to make his way toward the center of the room, but a servant lowered a silver tray in front of him. "Champagne, sir? It arrived from France only this morning."

"No, thank you." Simon stepped past the servant, his eyes on two young women in silk ball gowns against the wall. I have more serious business here than drinking champagne, he told himself.

Turning on his most charming smile, he slicked back his dark hair, tugged at his coat cuffs, and made his way to introduce himself to the two young women.

"Good evening," he said with a polite nod of his head.

The two young women, pale and blond with sparkling blue eyes, turned briefly to stare at him. Then, without replying, they returned to their conversation.

"Wonderful party," Simon offered, standing his ground, continuing to smile.

They ignored him.

"Allow me to introduce myself," he said, refusing to give up.

They walked away without another glance at him.

Such snobs! Simon sneered. There are so few wealthy people in this town that they all know one another. They stick together and do not allow any newcomers in. Especially newcomers with a northern accent.

The Haydn piece ended. After a brief pause the quartet began to play a reel. The room erupted excitedly as the young men and women quickly formed two long lines across the floor and began to dance.

Simon stepped into the line. He didn't know how to do this reel. But he was confident he could pick it up.

Confidence. That was the key, Simon knew. That was the key to being accepted by these wealthy New Orleans snobs.

As he picked up the rhythm of the dance, Simon attempted to catch the attention of the dark-haired girl across from him. She glanced at him briefly, then deliberately avoided him, keeping her eyes to the floor until the dance had ended.

I will triumph here eventually, Simon reminded himself. Young women will be begging me for a dance!

He made his way across the crowded, noisy room toward the central hall—and then stopped short in the doorway. A wide stairway, its banister festooned with yellow and white daisies, stretched up to his right. And standing on the bottom step, facing him as she leaned over the flowers, was the most beautiful girl Simon had ever seen.

She had black hair, lustrous in the gaslight from the chandelier above her head. Curls tumbled beside her face with clusters of flowers holding them in place. Simon could see her flashing green eyes, catlike eyes above a perfect, slender nose, dark full lips, high, aristocratic cheekbones, and the creamy white skin of her shoulders revealed above the lace-edged top of her blue ball gown.

A blue ball gown. Most of the other young women had selected pink and white and yellow. This one stood out boldly in satiny blue.

Simon moved closer, staring intently at this striking vision. He suddenly realized that his mouth was dry, his knees weak.

Is this what the poets call love at first sight? he wondered.

It was a feeling Simon had never experienced.

The young woman was still leaning against the banister, talking to another young woman, tall and frail looking in a gown of pink satin.

Look up. Look up. Please . . . look toward me, Simon urged silently.

But the two kept chattering, seemingly unaware of Simon's existence.

I must speak to her, Simon decided.

"What is her name?" He was so smitten, so stunned by the feelings sweeping over him, that Simon didn't realize he had spoken the question aloud.

"That is Henry Pierce's daughter, Angelica," an elderly man with a white mustache replied, eyeing Simon suspiciously. "Are you unfamiliar with our host and his family?"

"Angelica Pierce," Simon muttered, ignoring the man's question. "Thank you. Thank you so much."

Angelica Pierce, you do not know me, Simon

thought, dizzy with excitement, a kind of excitement he had never felt before. But you shall. You and I are meant for each other.

I shall introduce myself now, Simon decided, his heart pounding. He straightened his tailcoat and cleared his throat.

Continuing to stare intently at Angelica Pierce, he took two steps toward the staircase.

But he was stopped by firm hands on his shoulders.

Two grim-faced young servants had blocked Simon's path. "I am sorry, sir," one of them said coldly, a sneer contradicting his polite words. "But if you haven't an invitation, we must ask you to leave."

Chapter
2

"President Polk? He isn't here tonight —is he? You are teasing me, are you not, Angelica?" Liza Dupree gaped open-mouthed at her cousin.

Angelica laughed. "You are so gullible, Cousin Liza. What if I told you that the King of France were here? Would you believe that, too?"

Liza's cheeks reddened. "You are always teasing me, Angelica. You have such a cruel sense of humor."

"I do, *don't* I!" Angelica exclaimed, toying with a shiny black curl.

"You should have known President Polk wasn't here," Angelica told her cousin. "This party is much too exclusive. He would never get through the door!"

Both girls laughed.

"Did you see the gown Amanda Barton is wearing?" Angelica asked cattily.

"No. Is it charming and wonderful?" Liza asked.

"About as charming and wonderful as our window draperies," Angelica said with a sneer. "In fact, I believe it is made of the same fabric!"

Both girls laughed again. "I think this is the most wonderful party," Liza gushed. "I just adore—" She stopped when she saw she didn't have Angelica's attention. Angelica's gaze had flitted away for a second.

"Angelica, what did you see?"

"Who *is* that young man?" Angelica asked finally.

"Who? *Which* young man?" Liza asked.

"The one in the plain shirt and old-fashioned tailcoat," Angelica replied. "Don't allow him to see you looking. He is staring hard this way with big dark eyes."

Liza searched until she found him. "What an expression!" she declared, raising a hand to stifle her laughter. "Those brown eyes. He looks so sad and forlorn, like one of your father's hunting hounds!"

Liza expected Angelica to laugh, but she didn't. "Why is he staring at me like that?" Angelica demanded, stealing quick glances at him. "Do I know him?"

"I think I have seen his clothes on a scarecrow in one of my father's cotton fields!" Liza joked. "But I have never seen *him!*"

"He . . . he is frightening me," Angelica stammered. Her face suddenly appeared pale. The color faded from her eyes.

"Don't let him see us stare at him. He will surely come over here," Liza warned. "Shall we go upstairs for a rest?" She knew that Angelica was fragile, not as robust as she appeared.

"No. I— *Look!*" Angelica cried.

Both girls peeked as two solemn-faced servants stepped up to the young man. There was a brief argument. Then each servant grabbed an arm and forcefully pulled the young man toward the door.

"Oh, my! Oh, my!" Angelica cried, raising her hands to her pale cheeks.

Liza placed a hand on her cousin's shoulder. "It's all right."

A few girls cried out in alarm. Angelica heard a rush of murmured questions throughout the room. The string quartet stopped playing.

"He is leaving. It is all right," Liza assured her cousin.

Angelica watched as the young man moved toward the door, taking long strides, not turning back. As soon as he had disappeared, the music started up again.

"Just an intruder," Liza said. "I wonder how he got past the servants."

Angelica's expression was thoughtful. Her emerald eyes began to sparkle again. "That young man was rather interesting," she told her cousin. "There was something about him. . . ." Her voice trailed off.

"Angelica Pierce, I am ashamed of you!" Liza protested. "How can you be so selfish?"

"Selfish?" Angelica asked, raising her long skirt as she stepped down to the carpet.

"You already have not one but *two* handsome young men eager for your attentions. James Daumier and Hamilton Scott are two of the best-looking, wealthiest young men in all of New Orleans. And they would both *die* if they knew you found that shabby intruder interesting."

Angelica sighed. "Speak of the devil," she said, rolling her eyes. "Here comes James. It must be his dance."

"Well, go!" Liza urged, giving her cousin a gentle shove. "And *smile!* This is *your* party—remember?"

Angelica forced a smile and raised her eyes to James. James grinned at her, showing off about eight hundred teeth.

Does he have to grin at me like that? Angelica wondered unhappily. I am always afraid he is going to bite me!

Most girls would probably consider James Daumier good-looking, Angelica realized. He was tall and broad shouldered and had intense silver gray eyes beneath white blond hair.

If only he wouldn't grin like a dog that's just tucked away a juicy bone! Angelica thought.

"I have been looking all over for you. Were you and your cousin Liza gossiping about me?" James teased.

"We might have been," Angelica replied coyly.

She took his arm and allowed him to lead her to the dance floor.

He danced stiffly, standing three feet in front of her, his grin frozen on his face, his silver gray eyes staring into hers. "Are the musicians going to play that new dance?" he whispered, leaning closer. "The waltz?"

Angelica gasped and narrowed her eyes coyly at James. "James Daumier!" she cried. "You *know* my father would never allow evil waltz music to be played in this house! What a scandalous thought!"

James frowned in mock disappointment. "I have heard that it is quite an enjoyable dance."

Angelica started to reply. But James turned away as another young man tapped his shoulder. Angelica immediately recognized her other young suitor, Hamilton Scott.

"I believe this is my dance," Hamilton told James with a polite nod. James made an exaggeratedly formal bow and, flashing Angelica one last grin, backed away.

Hamilton had curly red hair and a face full of freckles. Angelica thought he looked about twelve. But he was nineteen, a serious young man with strong political feelings.

While James liked to talk to Angelica about fashion and friends and the sleek thoroughbred racehorses his father raised, Hamilton lectured her on the morality of slavery and the trade policies of the French.

"I wish you could dance every dance with me," Hamilton told her.

"I do not think my feet would survive it," Angelica teased.

She spent the rest of the evening dancing with James and Hamilton. She knew she should be having the time of her life. After all, it was Mardi Gras, and after this party there would be another party, and then another. But she found her mind wandering.

Something was troubling her.

When the party had ended and the last carriage clattered off into the night, Angelica walked past the servants busily cleaning up the ballroom and stepped through the French doors into the garden.

It was a cool night, the air soft and sweet smelling. Paper lanterns with oil lamps inside cast pale yellow light at her feet. A heavy dew made the grass glisten. Angelica bent and pulled off her satin party slippers. Holding them in one hand, she let her stockinged feet sink into the cool wet grass.

I should be thinking of James or Hamilton, she scolded herself. Then why does that intense-looking stranger keep filling my thoughts?

I am eighteen, Angelica thought. Father wishes me to marry soon. He is impatient for me to decide between James and Hamilton. He will make me marry one of them.

Do I love James? Do I love Hamilton?

I *like* them both, she told herself.

I like them both for different reasons. James for his good looks, his charm, his mischievous sense of humor. Hamilton for his intelligence, his serious-ness, his caring.

But do I *love* them? Do I want to marry either of them?

Deep in thought, gazing into the soft lantern light, listening to the rustle of the breeze through the magnolia blossoms, Angelica took a few steps into the garden.

She was too stunned to cry out when strong hands grabbed her from behind.

Chapter
3

Angelica gasped and spun out of her attacker's grasp.

"Do not cry out!" he whispered.

"Y-you!" Angelica stammered, her heart pounding. "Who *are* you? What are you *doing* here?"

"Do not be afraid. I will not harm you," Simon Fear whispered.

"But how did you get into my garden?" Angelica demanded, her fear turning to anger. "Who *are* you?"

"My name is Simon Fear," he told her, his dark eyes locked on hers.

Angelica bent to pick up her shoes, which in her alarm she had allowed to fall. But she kept her eyes trained warily on Simon. "You entered my party uninvited," she said, standing up. "Now you attack me in my garden. Are you a thief? Are you *mad?* What do you *want?*"

"I want you to marry me," Simon replied without hesitation. He pulled off his top hat and held it in front of him with both hands. His dark hair fluttered in the breeze.

Angelica started to reply, but only a startled laugh escaped her throat. "The answer is that you are *mad!*" she declared. "Will you turn and leave the way you came? Or do I have to call the servants to usher you out once again?"

"I saw you at your ball," Simon said, ignoring her questions, determined to tell her what was in his heart. "I saw you standing on the staircase. And I knew that I was in love with you."

"From one glance?" Angelica scoffed. "And how much champagne had you drunk, Mr. Fear?"

"Angelica, I knew at that moment," Simon continued, "that you would be my wife."

Angelica laughed again, but her laughter was tinged with fear. "Have you escaped from an asylum?" she demanded. "Are you dangerous? Can you hear a word I say?"

"You *will* be my wife, Angelica," Simon insisted, his dark eyes glowing in the lantern light.

"I am going to call for help now," Angelica told him, shivering. The hem of her long ball gown was wet. The wet grass had chilled her feet, and the cold ran up her body. "Please—"

"I will leave," Simon offered, still holding the top

hat in front of him. "I did not mean to alarm you. But I *had* to come back. I had to see you. To talk to you."

"You have said more than enough," Angelica told him dryly.

Simon replaced his hat and began running toward the back fence, the fence he had climbed to enter the garden. Halfway there he turned back to her. "You will marry me, Angelica Pierce. Mark my words!"

As he climbed the fence and vanished from the garden, her scornful laughter rang in his ears.

Simon wandered dizzily through town. The Mardi Gras parade had ended, sending hundreds of costumed revelers into the streets. Lively dance music, the *strump* of banjos, and the happy cries of fiddles and harmonicas poured from every doorway.

Torches floated by, casting a wash of eerie yellow light over the shouting, laughing faces. A group of masked partygoers rolled a barrel-size keg of beer along the side of the street. Several bare-chested men, weaving arm in arm ahead of Simon, sang a sad song at the top of their lungs.

Simon didn't see any of it.

As he made his way aimlessly through the whooping, laughing crowds of the French Quarter, all he could see was Angelica Pierce.

Dazed and nearly delirious with happiness, he wandered until he left the noisy crowds behind. All torchlight disappeared. This old section of town was dark, lit only by the sliver of moon overhead.

Where am I? Simon asked himself, noticing for the first time the low wooden buildings, all dark and silent. I seem to have wandered down by the docks.

The darkness brought darker thoughts to his mind.

Angelica, he had seen, already had suitors. *Two* suitors, to be exact.

After he had been removed from the party, Simon had doubled back and found a hiding place in front of the house. From his vantage point he had spied into the ballroom window.

Staring into the brightness, he had watched Angelica dance. He had seen the two young men who were her partners. Simon didn't know their names, but he would make it his business to find out.

Two worthy young gentlemen, Simon thought bitterly. But I am more worthy! I may not have their money or breeding—but I shall have Angelica!

His heart still pounded with the excitement of meeting Angelica. The dark streets appeared to tilt up to meet him. The low buildings grew darker. Behind the buildings he could hear the rush of water.

The docks must be on the next block, he realized. I have wandered into an unsafe neighborhood.

Just as he had this thought, he felt a heavy arm take hold of him. He felt a sharp pain as something sharp was pressed against his throat.

Chapter

4

Simon tried to cry out, but the pressure against his throat made him gag. It took him a few seconds to realize it was the blade of a knife pressed against his neck.

"I'll be taking your purse," a raspy voice whispered close to his ear, so close Simon could smell the whiskey on his attacker's breath. "Or I'll be cutting your throat."

Simon croaked out a helpless protest.

"A fine gentleman like you doesn't want his throat cut," the man rasped. *Does he?"* Then the attacker eased back the knife blade just enough to allow Simon to speak.

"I-I'll pay you," Simon managed to choke out.

I cannot die on this lonely dark street, Simon

thought, his legs trembling, his heart thudding loudly. I can't die now—I have just met Angelica.

"I have but little money," Simon said in a trembling voice. "But I will give it all to you."

"Yes, you will—and quickly!" the thief ordered. He loosened his hard grip on Simon, then gave him a hard shove in the back.

Startled, Simon cried out and stumbled to his knees on the hard cobblestones. He glanced up to see his attacker, a dark-haired young man with a red bandanna tied across his forehead. He was swaying drunkenly, squinting hard at Simon.

"What are *you* looking at?" he rasped angrily at Simon. "Your purse, or I'll cut you now!" He waved the knife.

"I-I'm getting it," Simon stammered.

As he pushed his cape out of the way, a stud fell out of his shirtfront and Simon's silver pendant dropped into view. Simon never removed the pendant since his sister Elizabeth had given it to him back home in Wickham two years before.

With its three silver claws and mysterious blue jewels, the disk-shaped pendant had been in the Fear family for generations. A strange old fortune-teller named Aggie had told him all about the pendant and its powers. But Simon had resisted using it. He had no use for evil magic.

Climbing to his feet, Simon quickly grabbed the chain and started to tuck the pendant back into his dress shirt.

But the thief had spotted it. He raised his knife

menacingly, the long blade gleaming in the moonlight. "Do not try to hide the silver coin, mate," the man growled. He stretched out his free hand. "I will take it, too."

"It is not a coin," Simon protested. "It is a family memento. Worthless to anyone except me."

"Give it up!" the thief shouted impatiently.

Simon reluctantly stepped forward. Holding the silver disk tightly in one hand, he struggled to remove the slender chain from around his neck.

The silver disk felt warm in his hand and vibrated as he gripped it.

A gust of wind blew down the street, fluttering Simon's cape. He reached to hand the pendant to the thief.

But instead of dropping it, Simon suddenly shoved the disk hard into the man's face. The four dark jewels dug into his cheek.

The thief cried out, more startled than hurt.

"Hey—you *die* for that!" he cried, brandishing the knife.

Still gripping the silver pendant, Simon jumped back.

Dark blood trickled down the man's cheek from small puncture holes. With an angry snarl he came at Simon.

Simon dodged the knife.

The thief swayed, squinting hard, trying to keep his balance, cursing under his breath. He leapt forward again, forcing Simon back against a building wall.

A pleased grin slowly formed on the man's face as he realized he had Simon trapped.

He stepped forward, watching Simon's helpless attempts to move away from the wall.

And then he stopped.

A howl of pain escaped his lips. He let the knife drop to the ground and grabbed the sides of his face with both hands. "Help me! My face—it's on *fire!*" he screamed.

Even in the pale moonlight Simon could see the man's face darken, as if badly sunburned.

"Help me!" the man shrieked. "Oh, please!"

His back pressed against the wall, Simon stared in helpless horror as the man's face darkened more. Then blistered. The blisters popped open and began to seep.

The man's eyes rolled around. His hands flailed. His shrieks faded to whimpers as the blistered skin burned away.

Chunks of skin melted off, revealing gray bone underneath. Gasping in agony, the man continued to whimper until no skin remained. A gray skull, locked in a hideous grin of horror, stared pitifully at Simon.

And then the body crumpled to the ground.

His chest heaving, the blood throbbing at his temples, Simon swallowed hard, forcing back his horror at the gruesome sight.

Then he carefully slipped the chain around his neck and tucked the ancient pendant under his dress shirt.

27

I have used the power of the ancient amulet, he realized. The Fear family has long had powers, powers it has used for evil, powers it has used for so many generations in its battle against the Goodes.

Dominatio per malum. Those were the Latin words engraved on the back of the silver disk. *Power through evil.*

Simon had long resisted the evil power of the Fear family. He had vowed never to use the ancient power of the pendant. The Goode family had been defeated. The centuries-old feud between the Goodes and the Fears was over.

Aggie, the fortune-teller, had told Simon his family would end in fire. The family name had been Fier then. "Rearrange the letters in Fier and you've got *Fire!*" the old woman had exclaimed.

Simon was determined that this prediction would never come true.

So he had changed his name from Fier to Fear. He wore the ancient evil pendant—but never used it.

Until this dark Mardi Gras night.

Wild thoughts raced through Simon's mind as he stared down at the dead figure crumpled at his feet.

I have the powers of the Fears, he realized. I have the power to get what I want. And what do I want most in the world?

I want Angelica Pierce. Beautiful Angelica.

Two obstacles stand in my path, Simon thought excitedly. Two obstacles—the two young men I saw dancing with her.

It shall be easy to get them out of my way, he

decided, feeling the warmth of the pendant against his chest.

The two young men have wealth and breeding. But I am a Fear. And what good are wealth and breeding *if you are dead!*

Having decided on his course of action, Simon swept his cape around himself. Then, stepping over the thief's body, he started toward home, humming happily to himself.

Chapter
5

"I love being up so high," Angelica told her cousin. "You can see everything from here."

"You can see everyone come in," Liza agreed, peering down at the orchestra seats through the ivory-plated opera glasses. "You can spy on everyone and gossip about them—and no one can hear you!"

Angelica laughed and tried to snatch the opera glasses from her cousin. James Daumier tugged at his cravat and shook his head disapprovingly. "The opera house is a place for beautiful music. Surely you do not come here to gossip."

"Look at that scarlet cape Margaret Fletcher is wearing!" Angelica exclaimed, ignoring James's comment. "It looks like something she should wear to the Mardi Gras parade."

"The color scarlet becomes Margaret Fletcher. She should wear it always," Liza said cattily.

James turned to Angelica. She could feel his silver gray eyes studying her. "Angelica, you look beautiful tonight."

"Oh, James, you're so sweet," Angelica replied. She squeezed his hand, but her attention was on the crowd filing into their seats in the orchestra below.

James leaned close. "Maybe some day you and I shall have an opera box of our own," he whispered.

"Why, James—what on earth for?" Angelica declared. "We can always use Father's. He *hates* the opera!"

"I meant—" James started, but stopped. Out of the corner of her eye Angelica saw his face go red.

Why is James so serious tonight? she wondered. Is he getting ready to propose to me? Is that why he seems so nervous and uncomfortable? Or is his cravat too tight?

If he *does* propose to me, what will be my reply? Angelica asked herself. She pulled up her long lacy white gloves and turned back to her cousin. "Liza, who are you looking at?"

"That young man from Biloxi," Liza replied without lowering the opera glasses. "The tall one with the charming smile and those devilish blue eyes. Remember, Angelica? You promised to introduce us?"

"Do you mean Bradford Diles?" James asked

Liza. "You wouldn't like him. He is not your type. He is witty and charming."

"What?" Liza's mouth dropped open in mock outrage.

James and Angelica laughed.

"I do not find your sense of humor at all amusing," Liza replied, making a sour face.

"I know you well," James continued. "You like the strong, silent type."

"I would like *you* better if you were silent!" Liza declared.

Angelica leaned over the velvet-covered railing to watch the people below. Rows of gaslights flickered brightly along the wall. The orchestra tuned up in the wide pit beneath the shimmering royal blue curtain. Dark-uniformed ushers led the lavishly dressed opera patrons to their seats.

Two weeks had passed since Angelica's ball. Two weeks of nonstop celebration and Mardi Gras parties.

One party with James, then one party with Hamilton, she thought. Then one party with both of them competing for her attention, for her smiles. James and Hamilton. Hamilton and James.

Who will it be? The question troubled Angelica, lingered in her mind like a headache that refused to go away.

On two occasions that strange, dark-eyed young man, Simon Fear, had come to call on her at her house. The first time she ordered the servants to send him away. The second time she agreed to see him—but made sure that Liza was in the room.

Simon had burst into the sitting room eagerly, a triumphant smile on his handsome face—as if being admitted to the house were an important victory for him.

He strode confidently up to Angelica, took her hand, and kissed it. Angelica heard Liza gasp, shocked by the young man's bold behavior.

The visit had been a short one since there was no adult available to chaperon. Angelica introduced Simon to her cousin. Simon greeted Liza warmly, then ignored her, rudely staring the whole while into Angelica's eyes.

As they talked of the weather and the Mardi Gras and other acceptable topics, Angelica remembered their brief but heated conversation that night in the garden.

"You will *be my wife,"* Simon had told her.

Every time the words repeated in her mind, every time she thought of his intense dark eyes and the confidence, the arrogant confidence in his voice, Angelica felt a chill of excitement—and fright.

When Simon had left, Liza tossed back her head and laughed. "What an absurd young man!" she declared scornfully. "Did you see the way he looked at you?"

"He has lovely eyes," Angelica replied.

Liza cut her laughter short, her expression suddenly serious. "Angelica, you cannot possibly be thinking about Simon Fear. Your father would have a *fit* if he knew you allowed Simon in this house! He would have the boy horsewhipped and sent back North to his home. Your father would never approve of Simon Fear—and neither should you."

Liza's words brought a smile to Angelica's face. "I do *not* approve of him," she told Liza. "I do not approve of him at all. . . ."

The orchestra stopped tuning up and fell silent. The gaslights were dimmed.

The Pierce family box was near the stage, high above the orchestra. It was the perfect place to see and be seen, which in Angelica's mind was the main reason to attend the opera.

James smiled at her. "It is about to begin. You and your cousin will have to stop gossiping for a while."

"Oh, good heavens! Look who is here!" Liza exclaimed. She handed the opera glasses to Angelica, then pointed below them.

"Who is it?" Angelica asked, raising the glasses to her eyes. "Oh!" Angelica uttered a soft cry of surprise as in the dimming light she spotted Simon Fear. He was in a seat beneath her box—staring up at her!

Realizing that her glasses were trained on him, Simon smiled wide and waved up at her.

Angelica lowered the glasses and sank back in her seat. "Such arrogance!"

Liza tossed her head. "The opera is supposed to be for society people," she said snootily.

"Who is it?" James asked Liza. "Have you found yourself another young man from Biloxi?"

"It is just someone I know," Angelica replied.

Something about Angelica's tone of voice roused James's curiosity. "Someone you know? A boy?" He leaned forward and peered down, his hands on the railing.

"James, please," Angelica whispered. "The opera is about to begin." She reached out to pull him back.

But to her surprise James rose to his feet, still leaning over the railing.

"James—what on earth—!" Angelica whispered.

James turned to her, his silver gray eyes wide in an expression of terror. His hands came off the railing. They rose stiffly in front of him, and he turned and started climbing onto the box railing.

"James—come down!" Liza shrieked. "James— get *off* there!"

James balanced awkwardly on the balcony railing for a moment, his mouth open in a silent scream. His arms began thrashing wildly at his sides. His legs trembled.

"James, you're going to *fall!*" Angelica cried.

She grabbed for him with both hands.

Too late.

Without uttering a sound, he toppled over the rail.

"James! James!" Angelica shrieked, her arms still outstretched.

She called his name again and again, not believing her eyes. Not believing that he was gone. Not believing the empty space beside her.

And then her high-pitched screams blended in with the other startled cries and shrieks of horror that filled the darkened hall.

Chapter
6

Simon watched the body plunge from the box. It hit with an echoing *thud* in the aisle.

Then, as horrified screams rose up in the darkness, Simon tucked the silver pendant under his dress shirt and quickly made his way to the aisle.

A few moments later he entered the private box to find Angelica and her cousin comforting each other, their tearstained faces filled with disbelief.

Liza's shoulders heaved as she sobbed. Her face was buried in her gloved hands.

Angelica gazed up, startled to see Simon. She brushed away the tears from under her eyes.

"I am so sorry for you, Angelica," Simon said softly, his dark eyes locked sympathetically on hers. "So sorry . . . so sorry."

"Did you—did you *see* him fall?" Angelica asked Simon. "Is James alive? I cannot bear to look."

Simon lowered his head sadly. "I am so sorry, Angelica. Your friend is dead."

"Nooooo!" Angelica uttered a wail of horror.

"He fell so far, so rapidly," Simon reported in a whisper. "I saw him land on his head. I am sure he died instantly."

Angelica shuddered and shut her eyes.

"He did *not* jump!" Simon heard Liza cry in a shrill, frightened voice. "Why would James jump? Why did he climb onto the railing?"

"If I can be of any help . . . " Simon offered Angelica, his hand placed lightly on her trembling shoulder. "Please know that you can always rely on me."

Angelica leaned against her father and allowed him to lead her into the sitting room. As they walked, she pulled off her black bonnet and tossed it onto a chair.

"It was a good funeral," Henry Pierce said in his gruff rumble of a voice. He was a burly, red-faced man with a thick black mustache, and his appearance was as gruff as his voice. "Until the horse pulling the hearse cart tossed a shoe. I cannot understand why they do not inspect these horses before a funeral starts."

"Yes, Father," Angelica replied weakly. She made her way to the long couch and sat down.

"You look very pale," her father muttered, narrowing his blue eyes as he studied her. "I wish you were stronger, Angelica."

"Yes, Father."

"You have stood up very well under this tragedy," he remarked, shaking his head sadly. He tsk-tsked, his mustache rolling up and down. "James Daumier was a fine young man."

Angelica sighed. She wished she could change her dress. The heavy black wool was hot and uncomfortable.

"Hamilton Scott will be a very suitable husband for you," Mr. Pierce said, striding to the window. "I have spoken to his father, who approves the match wholeheartedly."

"Father, please do not force me to think about marriage now. Not on the day of James's funeral," Angelica said in a quivering voice. "I feel so light-headed and fluttery. I am afraid I may swoon again."

"Save your strength, daughter. We will discuss it when you are feeling stronger." Mr. Pierce pulled back the window curtains. Bright yellow sunlight streamed into the room.

Angelica blinked, waiting for her eyes to adjust to the brightness. "Ah, Liza—here you are!" she cried, turning to the door.

Liza entered the room unsteadily, her black bonnet still covering her head, the hem of her black dress grazing the floor. "Funerals are so sad, Angelica!" she wailed.

"The funeral of a fine young man is especially sad," Mr. Pierce agreed solemnly. "Would you girls care for tea? I shall alert the staff."

Angelica watched as her father left, her hands folded tightly in her lap. "It—it was a pretty funeral," she stammered, motioning for Liza to sit down beside her. "All those flowers."

Liza pulled off her long black gloves and let them fall to the floor. She sat down beside her cousin and put a hand gently on her arm. "How are you, Angelica?"

"I feel better now that Father has left my side," Angelica admitted, covering Liza's hand with hers. "He means well, but he cannot stop talking about Hamilton Scott."

"You mean—"

"I mean with James *dead*—" The word caught in Angelica's throat. "With James dead," she started again, "Father is urging me to accept Hamilton. Father thinks it best that Hamilton and I announce our betrothal and marry as quickly as possible."

"But do you *care* for him, Angelica?" Liza asked.

Angelica replied with a pained sigh. She squeezed her cousin's hand. "Simon has been such a comfort these past few days," Angelica offered, focusing on the window. "He has been so considerate, so understanding."

"Angelica!" Liza exclaimed, unable to conceal her disapproval. "I had no idea you were seeing Simon Fear."

"He has paid me visits," Angelica said, still avoiding her cousin's stare. "He has been very kind. I do not know why you are so suspicious of Simon, Liza. Just because he is a northerner and does not come from wealth—"

"I do not trust him. That is all," Liza replied sharply. She shifted her weight on the couch. "You avoided my question about Hamilton. How do you feel about Hamilton, Angelica? Do you care for him?"

Before Angelica could reply, the butler appeared in the sitting room doorway. "Mr. Hamilton Scott is here," he announced. "Shall I show him in, miss?"

Simon Fear leaned against the white picket fence and stared at the sprawling mansion. From his vantage point Simon could see clearly into the sitting room window.

How considerate of Mr. Pierce to pull the curtains back for me, Simon thought.

A carriage came clattering by, pulled by two handsome black horses. Simon bent and pretended to clean something off his boot. When the carriage had passed, he took his place again beside the fence.

He saw Hamilton Scott enter the room and make his way to the couch where Angelica and Liza were seated. Hamilton bowed low and kissed Angelica's hand.

How very gallant you are, Hamilton, in your

boyish way, Simon thought cruelly, feeling the three-clawed pendant heat up under his shirt.

How unfortunate for you, Hamilton, that the next funeral will be yours. And then *I* shall be the one in the sitting room, bowing low to kiss dear Angelica's hand.

Chapter
7

One month later Angelica was holding on to Hamilton's arm as they pushed their way through the laughing, celebrating crowd. "Wait for me! My shoe is caught in a plank!" Liza called.

Angelica called impatiently back to her cousin. "Hurry! We don't want to miss Aunt Lavinia!"

"And I want to get a good look at this paddle-wheel boat!" Hamilton declared.

Liza managed to get her shoe free from the dock and moved quickly to her cousin, holding up the hem of her long gray dress.

"Do you see Aunt Lavinia?" Angelica asked. "There are so many people here to see the boat off, it looks like Mardi Gras all over again!"

As they moved closer to the boat, Angelica could see that a red carpet had been spread down the gangplank. Smiling passengers, their arms loaded with farewell presents, stopped on deck to wave goodbye to friends and family on shore.

A brass band played march music beside the gangplank. White and yellow streamers had been strung along the top of the pier. Horse-drawn taxis pulled up to let off more passengers.

"There she is!" Liza exclaimed. "Aunt Lee! Aunt Lee!"

Angelica and Hamilton pushed past a man pulling an enormous black steamer trunk and hurried up to greet Angelica's aunt Lavinia.

"Why, *there* you are!" Aunt Lavinia cried happily. "My goodness. I thought I missed you!"

Angelica's aunt was a large, robust-looking woman. Her blue traveling bonnet matched the blue of her eyes. Her round cheeks were flushed with excitement. She had traveled to New Orleans for Mardi Gras, but now was returning home to Memphis.

There were hugs all around. Angelica introduced Hamilton, who said something, but his words were drowned out by an ear-shattering blast from the boat whistle.

"Oh, my, I had better be boarding!" Aunt Lavinia exclaimed. "It was so nice of you to see an old aunt off!"

More hugs. Then Angelica's aunt gathered her belongings in her arms and started toward the gangplank.

"She is a dear," Liza said, waving to her aunt.

"This boat will make it upriver to Memphis in no time," Hamilton remarked. "Look. It has *two* paddle wheels. That should double its speed."

Another blast of the whistle made Angelica cover her ears. She tugged on Hamilton's arm. "There is no one on that pier," she said, pointing. "Come on. We can get a better view when the boat pulls away. We shall be right on the water."

Liza hesitated. "That pier is roped off, Angelica. I do not think they want us to stand there."

"We can stand there if we want," Hamilton said. "Come on. I want to be as close as I can when the boat starts to move."

With Hamilton in the lead, the three of them ducked under the rope and stepped out to the edge of the pier. Below them the water lapped against the wooden pilings, the water green and golden, shimmering in the bright afternoon sunlight.

"I can see fish down there. Look. A whole school of them," Hamilton said, bending over the edge of the pier and pointing into the gently rocking water.

"I—I don't think we should be here," Liza stammered. She glanced around uncomfortably.

"No one cares if we watch from here," Angelica told her cousin.

The last passenger had boarded, Angelica saw. The gangplank had been pulled on board. Two young sailors in white suits were rolling up the red carpet. The band started braying out another march.

Angelica shielded her eyes with one hand and

searched the deck for her aunt. She felt a tap on her shoulder. "Turn around," Liza instructed in a hushed voice. "Look who is here."

Confused, Angelica followed her cousin's gaze. To her surprise, Simon Fear was standing at the edge of the crowd. He had a hat pulled down over his forehead. His hands were stuffed into the pockets of a gray coat.

How strange, Angelica thought, staring intently at him. Why is Simon here? He doesn't appear to be seeing anyone off.

With two short blasts of its whistle, the paddle boat began to pull away from the dock, its wheels spinning slowly, churning the water.

Peering back toward the crowd, Angelica saw Simon pull something from his coat pocket. The silvery object caught the light of the sun. Simon raised the object high.

Angelica shook her head, then turned to watch the boat depart. What a strange young man he is, she thought, an amused smile spreading across her face.

Another blast of the whistle. The boat began to pick up speed. Behind Angelica the crowd waved and cheered.

Angelica watched the twin paddle wheels turn, creating two frothy waterfalls as the boat pulled away. She glanced back. Simon hadn't moved. He still held the silvery object high in one hand.

"Hamilton, this is exciting, isn't it?" she asked. "Hamilton? Hamilton?"

He had been standing by her side at the edge of the pier.

Where had he disappeared to?

"Liza, have you seen Ham—" Angelica started.

But her voice caught in her throat as she glanced back at the boat.

And then she started to scream.

Chapter

8

"Did he fall?" Liza cried. "Did he fall?" She grabbed Angelica, repeating the question. "Did he fall?"

"Hamilton! Hamilton!" Angelica screamed, raising her hands to her cheeks.

She watched Hamilton disappear under the golden green water.

And then she saw him rise up again as if floating on air.

"Hamilton! Hamilton!"

As Angelica gaped in horror, she saw that Hamilton was caught in the blades of the paddle wheel.

"No! Oh, please—no!" she shrieked.

His limp body rose up, then made a loud crunching sound as it was crushed between the wheel and the boat. It plunged back into the water, then was dragged up again, only to be crushed with another loud *crunch*.

"Did he fall? Did he fall?" Liza repeated the question breathlessly, crazily, strands of her brown hair loose and blowing wildly about her head. Tears streamed down her face.

Hamilton disappeared under the water. Then his lifeless body rose again. His arms waved helplessly. His head, the skull crushed beyond recognition, rolled back, then forward as the wheel carried him into the boat again.

The water pouring off the big paddle wheel was pink, stained with Hamilton's blood.

"No! Oh, no. Please, no!" Angelica moaned, unable to take her eyes off the gruesome scene of horror.

"Did he fall? Did he fall?" Liza continued her stunned refrain, her eyes rolling crazily in her head.

Suddenly Angelica felt a firm arm around her waist.

Uttering a soft cry of surprise, she turned to see Simon at her side. "Simon!" she cried in a high voice she didn't recognize. "Simon, he—he—" She pointed to the boat.

"Poor Angelica," Simon said softly, holding her tightly. "Poor Angelica. You have suffered so much."

"Angelica, it is a pleasure to see you out of your mourning clothes," Henry Pierce said, smiling beneath his dark mustache. He gently placed a hand on her shoulder in passing. "You are feeling better?"

Angelica nodded but didn't return his smile. She smoothed her shiny black hair. "Two months have passed, Father. I felt it proper to end my mourning for Hamilton."

Mr. Pierce made his way to the window and peered out into the evening darkness. "An unhappy time," he muttered, more to himself than to her. He turned back to Angelica. "You are so pale, daughter."

"I am feeling better," Angelica told him. "At least the dreadful fainting spells have ended."

"You have been considering my advice?" he asked, keeping his gruff voice soft. His eyes searched hers, as if seeking her true feelings. "I really do believe that traveling abroad is a good idea for you now."

Angelica sighed. "I haven't had much time to think," she replied with some sadness.

"I hope you have not been too lonely since Liza returned home to Virginia?"

"I needed this time by myself," Angelica said, toying with her hair.

"Simon Fear has visited you often," her father remarked, frowning.

"Simon has been a true comfort," Angelica replied.

Mr. Pierce nodded thoughtfully. "I hope you have not encouraged that strange young man in any way." He took one more glance out the front window, then made his way back to where Angelica was sitting. "I am feeling quite tired this evening. I believe I shall retire."

"Good night, Father," Angelica said. She rose and planted a kiss on his broad forehead.

Startled by this unusual show of affection, Mr. Pierce turned bright scarlet. He smiled, wished her good night, and strode quickly from the room.

Smiling to herself, Angelica moved to the sideboard against the wall and bent to pull two silver goblets from the cabinet. She busied herself there for a few moments, then returned to the couch.

About half an hour later the butler entered the sitting room, carrying a small white card on a silver tray. "Mr. Fear wishes to see you, miss," he said, presenting Simon's card to her.

Angelica took the card and glanced at it quickly, unable to suppress a smile. She nodded to the butler. "I will see him."

Simon entered, holding his hat in one hand, his dark hair slicked down, a look of concern on his face. But his expression softened to happiness when he saw that Angelica had traded her black mourning dress for a light-colored gown.

Smiling at her, his dark eyes glowing in the soft light of the gas lamps, he crossed the room quickly, then bent and kissed her hand.

She motioned for him to sit beside her. Raising his coattails, Simon lowered himself to the couch. "Angelica—" he started.

But she raised a hand to silence him.

Her emerald eyes burned into his. "Simon, I will marry you," Angelica said.

He stared at her blankly. He swallowed hard.

"Simon, did you not hear me?" Angelica demanded. "I said that I will marry you!"

"I—I am so—so—" he stammered.

Angelica tossed back her head and laughed. "Why, Simon, I have never known you to be tongue-tied!"

Simon blushed. "My dear Angelica, I am so overcome with happiness that I am speechless!" He took her hand in both of his. "I am thrilled, Angelica. I am the happiest man in all of New Orleans! I am *bursting* with happiness, I swear it!"

Angelica jumped to her feet and walked quickly to the sideboard. "Simon, let us have a toast," she said happily. "A toast to our marriage, to our happiness."

She filled the two silver goblets from a silver pitcher. Simon crossed the room and took one of the goblets from her hand. "To years and years of wedded happiness!" he proclaimed, beaming at her.

The silver goblets clinked.

They stood in front of the sideboard, their goblets raised, their faces glowing in the soft gaslight.

Then, to Angelica's surprise, Simon's expression darkened. "I must tell you something now, dear Angelica," he said, lowering his voice to a whisper.

She gazed back at him expectantly, her eyes locked on his.

"I love you so much," Simon said. "So much . . . I would do anything for you." He hesitated.

"Yes, dear," Angelica replied impatiently. "What is it?"

"I was so determined to have you. Nothing . . . no one could stand in my way." Simon continued, his eyes sparkling now.

"Yes?"

He took a deep breath, then let it out. "I love you so much—so much—that I *murdered* James Daumier and Hamilton Scott to win you!"

Chapter
9

Simon stared hard at Angelica, waiting for her reaction to his words.

She gaped at him in stunned silence, the silver goblet trembling in her hand.

"Angelica," he said, his voice quivering with emotion, his eyes pleading with her not to be repulsed by his news, not to reject him because of what he had done. "Angelica, I murdered them for *you*. That is how powerful my love is. My love for you is so overwhelming that I was driven to *kill* for you! I beg you to understand!"

Angelica didn't reply. She raised the goblet to her mouth and took a sip. A drop of the dark wine trickled down her lip.

Finally she spoke. "You—you *killed* them?"

Simon nodded solemnly.

"But how?" she demanded in a tiny voice.

He hesitated. "I have powers," he said simply. His hand tightened nervously around the goblet. Holding his breath, he stared at her, waiting for her to react.

To his surprise, Angelica's cat eyes narrowed and she uttered a scornful laugh.

"Angelica—?" he cried.

"You?" she cried. *"You* killed them?" She laughed again, laughed until tears rolled down her cheeks. "You fool!" she declared, shaking her head. "It was not *your* powers that killed those two oafs! It was *mine!"*

"What?" It was Simon's turn to gape.

"I killed them!" Angelica exclaimed through her tears of laughter. "I did it, not you! I have practiced the dark arts since I was a child. I knew I would never be allowed to marry you while James and Hamilton were around. And I knew that night at my party that you and I belonged together!"

"But, Angelica—!"

She raised a hand to silence him. "I could not marry James or Hamilton. They were both innocents, both lacking in imagination, both lacking the evil it takes to enjoy this world. So I cast spells. I murdered them both, Simon. I made James leap off our opera box railing. I made Hamilton fly off the pier into the paddle wheel. I murdered them for *you—*for *us!"*

Simon swallowed hard in stunned silence. "I—I do not *believe* it!" he finally managed to choke out.

"We will combine our powers," Angelica declared, raising her goblet.

"Yes, yes!" Simon agreed, quickly recovering from his shock. "Yes, Angelica, my dear. Together, nothing can stop us from getting what we want!"

Angelica's smile faded. "Only one thing can stop us, Simon, my love. One very powerful thing—my father. He will never approve of you. He wants to send me to Europe to get me away from you."

"Come! Let us see him at once!" Simon cried, his dark eyes sparkling with excitement. He grabbed Angelica's hand and began to pull her.

"Simon, stop! Where are you taking me? We cannot see Father yet. We have no plan. Simon, we need a strategy!"

Ignoring her pleas, Simon pulled Angelica toward her father's bedroom. They stopped short in the doorway when they saw Henry Pierce lying sprawled on his back on the bedroom carpet.

His face was bright purple. His mouth was frozen open. His lifeless eyes gazed up at the ceiling like clouded glass marbles.

"Simon . . . I—I—" Angelica gripped Simon's sleeve. "Is he—dead?"

"The doctor will believe it was his heart," Simon said softly, unable to keep a smile from forming on his handsome face.

"No!" Angelica cried, dropping to her knees beside her father's dead body. "Father!" She raised her eyes slowly to Simon. *"You* did it? You did it for me?"

"For us, my darling," Simon replied. "I murdered your father before I came into the sitting room. I knew it was the only way we could be together."

"Oh, thank you!" Angelica cried, jumping up and throwing her arms around him. "We are wealthy now, Simon. We are wealthy—and free!"

They hurried back to the sitting room and raised their silver goblets. "Let us drink!" Angelica urged. "To us!"

She clinked her goblet against his. They both drank.

"Delicious," Simon declared. "So bitter and sweet at the same time." He smiled at her knowingly. "It isn't wine—is it?"

"No," Angelica replied, returning his grin. "It isn't wine. It is blood."

Simon snickered and stared into the goblet. "You are full of surprises tonight, Angelica."

He wrapped an arm around her slender shoulders. Then they tilted the goblets to their lips and drank, allowing the rich, dark liquid to flow down their chins.

Village of Shadyside
1900

Nora Goode dropped the pen and tried to stretch the cramps from her aching fingers. Yawning, she stared at the narrow window on the bare gray wall.

Morning sunlight cast a small yellow rectangle over the dark floorboards.

Soon they will be coming, Nora thought, turning her eyes to the door.

I must finish my story before they come. I must leave this written record for all to see.

The evil that has followed the Fear family through the generations must be known. Otherwise it will never stop.

She raised the crust of bread from the metal pan of food that had been left for her and dipped it into the cold, yellowish gravy. Stuffing it hungrily into her mouth, she glanced at the stack of pages on the small desk.

So much more to write, she thought, picking up the pen and dipping it into the half-empty inkwell. The story of Simon Fear is so long and so frightening.

Simon and his precious Angelica were married in 1846. Now I must move my story to nearly twenty years later.

It is the year 1865. The War Between the States is drawing to a close.

Simon and his bride have moved North to Shadyside Village, where they built an enormous mansion in the woods, away from prying eyes. They used Angelica's money, of course.

They lived there with their five children: two daughters, Julia, seventeen, and Hannah, sixteen, and three sons, Robert, fourteen, Brandon, eleven, and Joseph, the youngest at five.

The family seemed happy and prosperous for a while. But with so much evil lurking within the walls of the Fear mansion, their happiness could not last.

Nora scraped the last of the yellow gravy from the pan. Then she picked up her pen, bent over her pages and began writing feverishly. . . .

PART TWO

Shadyside Village
1865

Chapter
10

"Whom will I be seated next to at the party tonight, Father?" Julia asked her father.

Simon Fear glanced up from the documents he had been reading. "Hmmm. I believe I have you seated next to the mayor, Julia."

"Oh, no!" Julia leapt up from her chair by the fireplace and marched purposefully to her father, who sat behind his small writing desk. "Please, Father. Must I sit next to Mayor Bradford? You know the man is completely deaf! He cannot hear a word anyone says to him!"

"Then that makes him the perfect dinner companion for you, my dear Julia," Simon replied cruelly, frowning over his square spectacles. "You never utter a word at our dinner parties. You always sit in complete silence. So you and the mayor should be perfectly content!"

"Father!" Julia uttered an exasperated cry.

Simon studied his oldest daughter with some sadness. She had her mother's beautiful black hair. But Julia's face was plain, her jaw too wide, her nose too long, her tiny gray eyes set too close together.

She was quiet, withdrawn, and shy, with little personality. A disappointment to Simon. He had hoped that moving to Shadyside Village, where the Fear family was the wealthiest and most prominent family, would help pull Julia from her shell. But she had become even more awkward and shy since the move.

She is only happy at her potter's wheel, Simon thought. Making vases and clay sculptures—that is the only time she smiles or shows any sign of enthusiasm.

"Father, I think you are being unfair to my sister!" Hannah came bursting in from the back parlor. "Julia can have my seat next to Mr. Claybourne. I am sure that she and that charming old man will find plenty to chatter about, if that is what concerns you."

Simon set down his papers and climbed to his feet. His back ached as he stood. He realized he was getting older.

He unfastened his stiff collar and pulled it off. "No, I am sorry. I want *you* to sit next to that windbag Claybourne," he told Hannah. "I want you to charm him, Hannah, as only you can. I need Claybourne's support for the library I wish to build."

With his eyes trained on Hannah, Simon didn't see Julia's hurt expression.

"I am sure that Julia could handle Mr. Claybourne as well as I," Hannah insisted, stepping behind her father's desk to give him a playful hug.

No, Julia could *not,* Simon thought. Hannah, he knew, was the charming sister. At sixteen she was tall, slender, and graceful, with wavy golden hair and lively brown eyes. She was as outgoing and lively as Julia was shy.

Simon needed his younger daughter at his dinner parties. He relied on Hannah to charm and delight the guests and to keep the conversation lively.

"The table is already set," he told the girls. He removed Hannah's arms from around his waist and straightened the papers on the little desk. "There will be no more discussion of this matter."

"Oh, Father!" Hannah complained with an exaggerated pout.

"I do not understand why we have so many of these endless, boring dinner parties, anyway," Julia said bitterly. "Can you not build all your libraries and museums and parks without so many dinner parties?"

"We have discussed this before," Simon replied impatiently. "I need the support of the important citizens of Shadyside. Why must I say all this again, Julia?"

Julia took a deep breath, struggling to keep back her tears. "Well, if you do not believe I have the personality to grace your table, if you really believe the only place for me is to be seated in the corner next to a deaf man, then perhaps I shall stay in my room tonight!" she cried.

Simon opened his mouth to reply, but a sound in the doorway interrupted him. He and the girls turned to see Mrs. MacKenzie, the housekeeper, enter with a short, red-haired girl in a maid's uniform.

"I am so sorry to be interrupting, sir," Mrs. MacKenzie said, rolling her white apron in her hands. "But I am training Lucy here on the procedure for dusting. Lucy is the new maid. She just started this week. She is helping us tidy up and get ready for the dinner party tonight."

Lucy blushed and lowered her eyes. She was a tiny girl, Simon saw. No more than eighteen. She had orangey red hair pulled back into a tight bun, pale green eyes, and a tiny, sharp nose like an upturned V.

"Go right ahead and dust, Mrs. MacKenzie," Simon said, happy that his discussion with Julia had been interrupted. "I am going upstairs now to speak with my wife about tonight."

"Now, Lucy, you be careful of Miss Julia's fine pottery here," Simon heard the housekeeper instruct as he nodded goodbye to his daughters and made his way to the front stairs.

"Father, I wasn't finished!" Julia called shrilly.

Simon ignored her and continued down the long marble-floored hallway. As he reached the stairway, his three sons, Robert, Brandon, and Joseph, came bounding down, dressed in their riding outfits.

"And where might you be going, as if I could not guess?" Simon asked.

"I am taking the boys for a short ride," Robert replied, straightening little Joseph's cap.

"My pony is waiting for me," five-year-old Joseph told his father.

"Be watchful in the woods," Simon warned Joseph. "My horse balked at a snake yesterday afternoon. Nearly threw me. I killed the snake, but there might be more."

"I'm not afraid of snakes!" Brandon declared. "I step on them!"

Robert gave his younger brothers a gentle shove toward the door. "Don't worry, Father. I will take care of them."

They went on their way, and Simon climbed the stairs, his mind on the dinner party just a few hours away.

At the top of the stairs a maid was polishing the mahogany banister. Simon stepped past her and hurried toward his wife Angelica's room.

"Angelica!" he called eagerly from the hallway. "Angelica, I have several matters to discuss with you, my dear."

He stopped in her doorway, his hands on the doorframe—and gasped.

"Angelica!"

Simon stared down at her. She was sprawled on the floor on her back, her black hair in disarray around her head, her green eyes staring blankly at the ceiling, her mouth open.

Angelica. Not breathing. Lifeless.

"Angelica!" Simon cried. *"Oh, Angelica!"*

Chapter
11

Simon's frightened cries aroused Angelica, and she sat up. She blinked once, twice, and smiled at him, her emerald eyes shining.

"Simon—where am I? What is happening?" she asked groggily.

"I—I found you on the floor, Angelica!" Simon replied, greatly relieved. "I thought you were—"

"The spirits," Angelica whispered, sitting up. "The spirits called me, Simon. I must have swooned, fallen into a trance."

"I was frightened," Simon said, taking Angelica's slender white hands and pulling his wife to her feet.

Angelica squeezed his hand affectionately. "I slip in and out of my trances and cannot control them as I used to."

She lowered herself to the edge of the bed, straightening her black hair with both hands. She looked tired. In the sunlight from the window he could see that her once smooth face was lined, the skin tight and dry. Only her eyes retained their youthful glow.

"Angelica, perhaps it is time to put away the magic, to retire your dark arts," he said softly, standing over her.

She gazed up at him in surprise. "Simon, my powers have served us well," she said. She gestured around the luxurious bedroom. "We have become even more wealthy, the wealthiest people in Shadyside. We have five wonderful children. We have succeeded because of our powers, yours and mine. I cannot give up now."

"But to enter your room and find you lying unconscious on the floor—" Simon started.

Angelica raised a hand to silence him. "When the spirits call, I must follow." She muttered a chant.

"Angelica—"

"Simon, hush. The spirits will hear you. I will have to cast a cleansing spell to rid the house of your negative words."

He sighed and paced the carpet in front of her. "Let us change the subject," he said finally. "Let us discuss the dinner party tonight. I have spoken to Hannah and Julia and—"

"I cannot attend the party. I am sorry, Simon," Angelica told him abruptly, climbing to her feet.

He turned, startled. His face reddened. "What?"

"I read the cards this morning," Angelica told him with a shrug. "They advised against any kind of celebration."

"Angelica, I beg of you," Simon said heatedly. "I need you this evening. As you know, this dinner party is most important."

"I am sorry," she replied, taking his arm. "I cannot go against the cards. I cannot take that risk. I cannot tempt the vengeance of the spirits. I must always obey. Ask one of the girls to act as hostess, Simon. I will stay in my room tonight. The cards have instructed me."

Simon sighed. He knew there was no point in arguing with his wife. He gazed at her with concern. Her dark powers had taken over her life, he realized. Her chants, her spells, her cards —they kept Angelica in her room for days at a time.

The children worried about her and missed her. And now Simon realized that he, too, was worried.

"Give the cards another reading, Angelica," he urged, handing the deck of strange, colorful cards to her. "Perhaps they will advise you differently this time."

"Very well," she replied softly, "but I know what they will tell me." Smiling, she gave Simon a gentle shove toward the door. "Go now, husband. Go ask Hannah to serve as your hostess. She will charm your guests even better than I."

Reluctantly Simon bid her farewell and made his way from her room. He could hear her murmuring over the cards as he walked along the long hall to the front stairs.

Simon was halfway down the stairs when he heard a loud, shattering crash from the parlor.

Chapter
12

"My favorite bowl!" Julia was screaming as Simon rushed into the parlor. "That was the best bowl I ever made!"

"I'm so sorry, miss," Lucy, the new maid, said quietly, staring down at the shattered pieces on the carpet. "It—it just slipped from my hand." She covered her face with her hands.

"What has happened here?" Simon demanded.

Julia bent to pick up the largest piece of her bowl. "Shattered," she said sadly, shaking her head.

"I *told* you not to hold it in one hand like that!" Mrs. MacKenzie scolded Lucy.

"Lucy has dropped Julia's favorite pottery bowl," Hannah told Simon. She walked over to Lucy and Mrs. MacKenzie. "I am sure you did not do it on purpose, Lucy. Go get a broom and clean it up."

"I *told* her not to hold it like that," Mrs. Mac-Kenzie repeated fretfully. She gave the trembling maid a shove. "Well, go on, girl. Let's be cleaning this mess up. And no more accidents, hear? We have a lot to do before the guests start to arrive."

Simon shook his head fretfully at Julia. "I am certain you can make another bowl just like it," he said impatiently. "We really have no time to worry about your pottery today."

Hurt, Julia started to reply. But Simon turned quickly to Hannah. "I will need you to be hostess tonight, Hannah. Your mother is . . . not feeling well."

The girls exchanged glances.

Hannah took her father's arm. "I shall be glad to take Mother's place tonight," she said. "But shouldn't Julia act as hostess? She is the oldest, after all."

Simon pulled away from her impatiently. "Please!" he cried sharply. "Enough arguments and discussion for today! I asked *you* to be my hostess tonight, Hannah. I do not believe any further discussion is necessary!"

Before either of his daughters could reply, Simon stormed out of the room.

Hannah turned to Julia, who still held a shard of pottery in her hand.

"Father has no confidence in me, I am afraid," Julia remarked sadly. She let the piece fall to the carpet.

"Julia, I feel so bad," Hannah said with genuine feeling. "But you know how Father is, so headstrong and stubborn."

Julia forced a smile. "Dinner parties make me so nervous. But perhaps I can be a success tonight. Perhaps I can force Father to change his mind about me."

In the kitchen Mrs. MacKenzie continued to scold Lucy. "Be careful, my girl," she warned. "You don't get many chances in this household."

"I will. I promise," Lucy replied meekly.

Mrs. MacKenzie handed the maid a long sheet of paper with several names scrawled on it. "Here, Lucy. You must sign the servants' list."

Lucy hesitated. "But I cannot write, ma'am," she said, blushing.

Mrs. MacKenzie took the paper from her. "Very well, then. Tell me your complete name, child, and I will scribble it for you."

"My name is Lucy Goode," the maid replied quietly.

Mrs. MacKenzie started to write, then stopped. Her eyes narrowed as she trained them on the girl. "Goode, did you say?"

Lucy nodded.

"Well, I wouldn't be repeating that name around here if I was you," the old housekeeper advised. "Mr. Fear is always talking about some family named Goode that done him wrong. Keep the name to yourself, girl. If you wish to keep your job."

"Don't worry," Lucy replied, her eyes suddenly cold and hard. "I won't be telling a soul."

As the guests arrived that evening, Hannah stood beside her father, her lively brown eyes reflecting her excitement. Her gown was made of delicate white lace over green satin. A hoop underneath made the wide skirt hold its shape. The skirt was three-tiered, the hem of each green tier trimmed with white lace.

Hannah wore short white lace gloves, and her gown had ruffled short sleeves. Her blond hair was tied to one side in a tight bun, held in place by a corsage of yellow and white flowers.

Julia's dress was simpler, white lace over pink velvet. The neckline dipped low, revealing her shoulders. Her shiny black hair, parted in the middle, fell gracefully in ringlets beside her face.

"You look wonderful tonight," Hannah whispered to her sister. She could see that Julia had taken extra care with her appearance. "Father is sure to notice," Hannah whispered, doing her best to encourage Julia.

Julia will never be a beauty, Hannah thought with some sadness. But when she dresses up, she looks quite lovely. If only she would smile more and not clasp her hands so tightly in front of her.

Wine was served in Simon's library. The large square room, furnished in dark wood furniture, with its four walls of bookshelves, seemed to be the perfect setting for an evening devoted to discussing the Shadyside village library.

Working hard to be a good hostess, Hannah moved from guest to guest, her eyes sparkling, her smile warm and genuine. She chatted and joked with Harlan Claybourne. She even managed to get a smile from sour old Mayor Bradford.

A short while later Simon led everyone to see his new collection of weapons and uniforms from the War Between the States. Simon had been collecting swords and rifles from both the armies of the North and the South. After admiring Simon's collection, they were all summoned to the formal dining room for dinner. Simon led the way with Hannah on his arm.

The majestic room was lighted entirely by candles. Silver candelabras glowing with tall, slender candles were placed every few feet along the center of the white Irish linen tablecloth. The silver dinner plates and delicate wineglasses shone in the soft, flickering light.

"You set a fine table, Simon," Harlan Claybourne declared grandly, taking his place next to Hannah.

"I have fine guests," Simon replied graciously.

Father is certainly in a good mood tonight, Hannah thought gratefully. She had seen him become sullen and silent at parties that weren't going as planned.

I do wish Mother were here, Hannah thought. She is ill so often lately. She spends so much time upstairs in her room that I am actually lonely for her.

Hannah watched as Julia helped the old mayor into his chair at the far end of the table. Then Julia took her lonely place beside him. The mayor immediately reached for the loaf of bread. He took a piece for himself, Hannah saw, and didn't even offer the bread to Julia.

Poor Julia, Hannah thought, lowering herself into her seat. Father can really be unfair at times.

She turned her attention to Mr. Claybourne and began chatting with him about his horses.

A few moments later Lucy entered in a starched black uniform with a lacy white apron over it, carrying a large china tureen of soup. Starting at the head of the table, she served Simon Fear first, dipping a long-handled silver ladle into the tureen and filling his bowl with the soup.

"Very good, Lucy," Simon said approvingly. "That is a very big tureen. Are you sure you do not need help with it?"

"No, sir," Lucy replied meekly. "Mrs. MacKenzie said I can do it on my own."

She continued down the table, ladling the rich orangey-red soup into bowls.

"What *is* this marvelous soup? Is it tomato?" Mrs. Graham, the reverend's wife, asked as Lucy continued down the table.

"It is lobster bisque," Hannah replied, "in a tomato base."

"It certainly is hearty," Reverend Graham remarked.

78

Hannah started to say something about the recipe but was interrupted by a high-pitched shriek from the end of the table.

It took Hannah a moment to realize that it was Julia who was screaming frantically at the top of her lungs.

Chapter
13

"My shoulder! Ohhhhh, my shoulder!" Julia shrieked.

Several guests cried out as Julia leapt to her feet, sending her chair clattering to the floor.

"I'm so sorry, miss!" Lucy cried, struggling to hold on to the big soup tureen.

"Owww! My shoulder! And look at my dress!" Julia wailed.

"My arm was bumped. I didn't mean to spill it!" Lucy backed timidly against the sideboard.

Julia grabbed up her white linen napkin and began dabbing frantically at her shoulder and the neckline of her dress. "Ow, it burns!" A dark orange stain ran down the white lace shoulder of the gown onto the pink velvet bodice.

"Julia, dear, you may be excused to freshen

yourself up," Simon called from the head of the table.

He intended to be understanding, Julia knew, but she heard only disapproval in his voice.

I have done something clumsy once again, Julia thought unhappily. Hannah would never have behaved so badly.

Hannah wouldn't have screamed and knocked her chair over, Julia knew. Hannah wouldn't have made such a commotion.

But what could she do? That steaming-hot soup really *burned!*

"Are you hurt, sister? Do you need help?" Hannah called from the other end of the table.

"No, I do not need help," Julia replied through clenched teeth. Disgusted with herself, she tossed the napkin onto the table, muttered "Excuse me," and started for the door. She could feel her face burning and knew she was blushing.

She glanced at the doorway and stopped short when she saw the expression on Lucy's face.

Was that a smile? A pleased smile?

Late that night, after the guests had boarded their carriages and headed home, after the servants had cleaned up, Hannah and Julia met in the secret room only they knew about.

It was a long, narrow room without windows, hidden behind the second pantry. Heat from the kitchen stove on the other side of the wall kept the small room cozy and warm. A small gas lamp cast a dim light.

The two sisters had discovered the room when they were small children and had used it as a secret meeting place ever since. They had sneaked blankets and feather pillows in and sometimes pretended they were girls hiding in a faraway cave.

That night Julia did not feel like discussing "little girl" things. Her back resting on a pillow propped against the warm wall, her hands clasped tightly in the lap of her wool nightdress, Julia sighed unhappily.

Beside her, Hannah yawned and tugged at a strand of fine blond hair.

"Did you not see Lucy's expression?" Julia demanded in a low whisper. They always whispered in this secret room, even though no one could hear. "Did you not see the smile on the maid's face?"

Hannah shook her head thoughtfully. "My eyes were on you, sister. It took me a while to see what all the commotion was."

"But afterward," Julia insisted impatiently. "After I jumped up and knocked my chair over, did you not see Lucy smile as if she were pleased about what she had done to me?"

"No," Hannah replied softly. "I only heard Lucy apologize."

"I *saw* her smile!" Julia exclaimed, raising her voice angrily. "She spilled the soup on my bare shoulder *deliberately!*"

"Why?" Hannah asked, gesturing for her sister to lower her voice. "I do not understand, Julia. *Why* would Lucy do such a thing? She has no reason to harm you."

Julia ignored her sister's question. "First she broke my finest work of pottery. She apologized for that, too, as I recall," Julia said bitterly. "And then she embarrassed me in front of Father, when I was trying so hard to . . . to act the way he wants me to. Did Father say anything to you? About *me?* About what happened?"

"He seemed displeased that there was a disturbance," Hannah replied, yawning again. "But I think Father was very happy about the dinner."

"Happy about *you,*" Julia muttered.

"Being hostess is such hard work," Hannah said. "I thought my smile would freeze on my face."

Lost in her own thoughts, Julia didn't appear to hear her.

"I am so tired," Hannah said, sighing. "I think we had better go up to our rooms."

"Yes," Julia agreed.

The two sisters climbed to their feet, leaving the pillows against the wall. Silently they started toward the door.

In the dark, empty pantry Julia stopped and grabbed Hannah's hand. "Just heed my warning, sister. Keep an eye on the new maid. Something about Lucy is not right."

Too tired to argue, Hannah muttered her agreement, and the two sisters proceeded up the dimly lit stairway to their rooms.

A single gaslight on the hallway wall provided the only light in the long corridor. As Hannah made her way to her bedroom, she saw Lucy silently slip out her door and vanish into the shadows.

How strange, Hannah thought, feeling chilled and afraid.

The servants have all retired. Why was Lucy in my room at such a late hour?

Curious, she stepped into the bedroom. Logs crackled pleasantly in the fireplace. Hannah's party dress had been removed from the chair on which she had tossed it. The bedclothes were neatly turned down.

How nice of Lucy, Hannah thought, sliding into the linen sheets. She felt a momentary pang of guilt for talking about the new girl with Julia.

I mustn't listen to Julia's wild accusations, she scolded herself.

Hannah pulled the goose-down comforter up over her shoulders and let her head sink into the pillow. Smiling to herself, she listened to the soothing crackle of the fire.

"Oh—!" she whispered when she felt something move against her bare leg.

It must be a wrinkle in the sheet, she told herself.

She shut her eyes again. She was so sleepy. She hoped she could fall asleep quickly.

"Oh—!" Hannah froze.

What was that?

Did something move? Is something in my bed?

She tried to cry out, but her voice caught in her throat as she felt something slither up her leg.

Chapter
14

―――――

Too frightened to scream, Hannah felt the warm creature slide over her leg. She forced herself not to move. Not to breathe.

It curled itself around her ankle. Then she felt it uncoil.

"Ohhh." She uttered a low, terrified moan and leapt from the bed.

In the flickering light from the dying fire she tossed back the bedclothes and searched the shadows of her bed.

She heard a *hiss,* then saw the flash of dark eyes.

"A snake!" she cried in a tiny, frightened voice.

Rising up on the wrinkled sheet, the snake arched its head and bared its pointed fangs, preparing to attack.

Hannah stood frozen in terror. "How did a snake get into my bed?" Hannah asked aloud. "How?"

Then, with a short cry, Hannah sprang into action and threw the covers over the hissing creature. And started to scream for help.

Hannah's brothers were blamed for the prank. They had been riding in the woods. They must have captured the snake and hidden it in Hannah's bed.

They all denied it. But Simon ignored their protests and punished them. He had little patience for jokes and pranks. "They do not lead anyone closer to success," he warned sternly.

The next evening Hannah was in her room dressing for dinner. Having pulled on a simple white linen frock, high-collared with a delicate red velvet ribbon at the throat, she brushed her long blond hair and tied it back with a matching red ribbon.

She heard a scrabbling at the door and turned to see Fluff, her tiny white terrier, prance into the room, a red ball clamped in his teeth.

"Not now. No ball playing," Hannah told the dog. "You will make me late for dinner, Fluff." She gave the disappointed dog a gentle shove toward the door.

Then she pulled open her wardrobe door to search for her white shoes. "Where *are* they?" she said, bending to search the bottom shelf.

Lucy had straightened Hannah's room that afternoon. She must have moved the shoes, Hannah thought.

She finally found them on the floor at the foot of her bed.

Holding on to the bedpost, Hannah balanced on her left foot and slid her right foot into the low pump.

"Ohhh!" she cried out as a sharp pain shot up her leg.

Looking down, Hannah was horrified to see bright red blood trickling over the white heel of the shoe.

As the sharp pain shot up from her foot, Hannah dropped to her knees on the bedroom floor and pulled off the shoe. Blood had already stained the inside of the shoe.

Hannah bent to examine her foot. Wiping away the bright trickling blood with her fingers, she found a deep cut nearly an inch long on her heel.

Stuck in the cut was a shard of clear glass.

"Oh!" Grimacing with pain, Hannah pulled the piece of glass from the cut with trembling fingers.

The blood flowed more rapidly from the open cut. Balancing on one leg, Hannah screamed for help.

Mrs. MacKenzie appeared a few seconds later. She guided Hannah to the bed. Hannah hopped on one foot, leaving a trail of blood. Then the housekeeper hurried out for gauze bandages.

"Hannah, what has happened?" Julia entered the room breathlessly, a frightened expression on her face. Seeing the trail of blood across the floor, Julia gasped.

"I'm all right, I believe," Hannah told her,

watching the blood flow from her heel. "I—I cut my foot."

"How?" Julia demanded, stepping over the blood-covered shoe to get to Hannah's bedside.

Hannah held up the piece of glass that she had kept tightly gripped in her hand. "It was in my shoe," she said, grimacing from a shot of pain that traveled up her leg.

"How dreadful!" Julia declared, staring at all the blood.

"Lucy cleaned my room today," Hannah added darkly. "I believe you may be right about her, Julia. She—" Hannah stopped as Mrs. MacKenzie returned with the gauze bandages.

Julia watched as the housekeeper expertly cleaned and then bandaged Hannah's injured foot. "The bleeding will stop soon," Mrs. MacKenzie assured Hannah, patting her shoulder as if she were still a little girl. "You will be able to come down to dinner in a few minutes. But I would not advise any long hikes for a few days, Miss Hannah."

Hannah thanked Mrs. MacKenzie. As soon as the housekeeper had left the room, Hannah turned back to Julia. "Lucy cleaned my room and moved my shoes. I believe you were right about her. She deliberately—"

Julia raised a hand to stop her sister's accusation. "Are you really sure that Lucy put the glass in your shoe?"

"Who else could have done it?" Hannah demanded impatiently, staring down fretfully at the bandaged foot. "We must tell Father at once. That girl must go. She must be dismissed today. She is a menace! Ow!" She cried out, feeling another stab of pain.

Julia lowered herself to the bed beside her sister and put a comforting arm around Hannah. "Try to calm yourself, sister," she said in a whisper. "We do not want to accuse Lucy if she is innocent."

"Innocent?" Hannah cried shrilly.

"We have no proof," Julia said, playing with Hannah's blond hair, soothingly braiding and un-braiding it as she had done when they were young-er. "We do not know that Lucy put the glass in the shoe."

"No one else was in my room!" Hannah ex-claimed.

"But the glass may have fallen from Lucy's dustpan," Julia said. "It may have been an acci-dent, a bit of carelessness."

"But, Julia—"

"I have my own suspicions about Lucy, as you know," Julia continued, ignoring her sister's pro-test. "But I do not think we should accuse her in front of Father until we have proof."

Hannah stared hard at her sister. Father is right about Julia, she thought with some sadness. Julia is too timid. She has no backbone. She is reluctant to stand up even to a servant girl.

But Hannah decided to back down. "Very well," she said softly. "I will give Lucy one more chance."

"Can you walk down to dinner, or will you need help?" Julia asked, getting to her feet.

"I can walk," Hannah replied softly. "Go ahead.

You know Father hates to be kept waiting for his dinner."

"Mother has actually left her room and is joining us tonight," Julia announced.

"How nice!" Hannah declared. "I shall be right down. Give me a few moments to brush my hair and straighten my dress."

As soon as Julia had left the room, Hannah gingerly climbed to her feet. She found that if she stepped lightly on her cut foot, standing nearly on tiptoes, she could walk with little pain.

Putting most of her weight on the uninjured foot, she made her way across the room to her small dresser mirror and began to brush her hair.

She had finished and set down the brush when she felt another presence in the room—someone to the side of her, staring at her.

Hannah spun around quickly and cried out in surprise.

Lucy was standing in the room, her cheeks bright red, a frightening wild-eyed expression on her face.

As Hannah shrank back against the dresser, Lucy darted forward quickly to attack her.

Chapter
15

Her cheeks scarlet, her eyes wild, Lucy stopped a few feet in front of Hannah, breathing hard.

What is she going to do to me? Hannah wondered, pressing against the dresser, her hands raised as if to shield herself from the maid's attack.

"Mrs. MacKenzie t-told me—" Lucy stammered, pointing down. "About your foot, I mean."

"Yes?" Hannah managed to utter in a tight, frightened voice.

"Well, I came up to see if there was anything I could do. To help, that is."

"I think you've done *quite* enough," Hannah replied coldly.

Lucy appeared stung by Hannah's words.

Hannah immediately felt sorry.

Lucy was red-faced and breathing hard because she had hurried up the stairs to help me, Hannah realized. I have become so frightened of her, so suspicious of her, that I really believed she had come to attack me!

"I am sorry you are in pain, miss," Lucy said, lowering her eyes to the floor. "If there is anything I can do for you . . ."

"Thank you, Lucy," Hannah replied, softening her tone. "You may clean up the floor. There was quite a lot of blood. Then take that shoe down to Mrs. MacKenzie. Ask if there is any way it can be cleaned."

"Yes, miss," Lucy said, still avoiding Hannah's gaze.

Limping gingerly, Hannah made her way past Lucy and headed downstairs to dinner.

The picnic was Hannah's idea. She had been cooped up in the house for three days nursing her injured foot. Now the foot was nearly healed, and she was walking normally.

"What an excellent idea," Julia said brightly. "I shall have a basket lunch made up. We shall go out to the woods and enjoy this beautiful day."

Joseph, Brandon, and Robert begged to come along. "I promise we won't be any trouble," begged Robert. "And I shall watch Brandon and Joseph carefully."

Fluff also seemed excited by the idea. The little

dog leapt eagerly at the pantry door, whimpering to go out into the sunshine.

"Go get dressed," Julia instructed her sister. "I shall go speak to Lucy about preparing our lunch basket."

The mention of Lucy's name gave Hannah a chill. She had avoided the maid for three days. Hannah realized that she was perhaps being unfair. Lucy *couldn't* be deliberately trying to hurt the two Fear sisters. What reason could she have?

Just the same, Hannah had decided to avoid Lucy and to have as little to do with her as possible.

Pushing Lucy out of her mind, she hurried upstairs to get changed for the picnic.

"Why do they call it Indian summer?" Brandon asked.

"I am not sure," Hannah told him. "But today is certainly the most beautiful Indian summer day."

The sun was high, seeming to float above tiny puffs of white cloud. Leaves shimmered brightly on the tall trees at the back of the lawn. They were still summer green although autumn was here.

Despite the sunshine, the air carried a chill. Hannah wrapped her light blue shawl around her as she watched Fluff scamper through the tall grass.

"Joseph, don't chase Fluff!" Julia ordered. "You're getting the poor dog all excited!"

"I am afraid that Fluff is already excited," Hannah told her, laughing as the dog rolled onto its back and frantically kicked at the air with all four paws. Joseph rolled on the ground, imitating the dog.

"Robert, hold the picnic basket straight. You are going to spill everything!" Julia cried.

"But it is so *heavy!*" Robert complained. "What did Lucy pack in here—an elephant?"

"The flowers are beautiful," Hannah said, pleased to be out of the house. "Look, Julia, we still have roses."

Julia didn't reply. She was distracted by Fluff and Joseph. "Joseph!" she called. "Look out! Do not let the dog fall into that hole!"

At the edge of the woods they all stopped to watch Fluff as he neared a burial plot.

With Joseph close behind, the dog ran to the edge of the freshly dug grave, sniffed along the sides at the moist, dark dirt, then came trotting back toward Robert, Brandon, and the girls.

"Why is there a new grave?" Robert asked, shifting the heavy picnic basket to his other hand, his eyes on the deep hole.

"Did you not hear about Jenkins, the gardener?" Julia asked. "He passed away in his sleep two nights ago. He is to be buried this afternoon."

"Such a kindly man," Hannah said softly. "And look at his fine work all around." She gestured to the flower garden that stretched along the back of the house, bordered on one side by tall rose trellises.

Hannah stepped closer to the grave, staring down into the deep rectangle of dark earth. How strange to think that Jenkins was walking around in our yard just two days ago, she thought with some sadness. And in a short while he shall rest in this underground hole—forever.

"Remove that solemn frown from your face, sister," Julia urged, stepping up beside Hannah. "Let us not allow this to spoil our fun today."

Hannah forced a smile and turned away from the grave. "Yes, you are right. Into the woods, everyone!" she called brightly and started to run toward the trees, her blue shawl flapping behind her gingham dress.

The woods behind the Fear mansion seemed to stretch on forever. The five picnickers ran into the shadows of the tall trees. Their heavy shoes made the twigs on the ground crackle and snap.

"It's almost cold here under the trees!" Hannah exclaimed.

"How far do we have to walk? This basket is heavy!" Robert complained.

"We can set it down when we come to a clearing," Julia told him.

"Look at Fluff!" Joseph cried, pointing.

The dog had chased a squirrel up a tree and was now trying to climb the trunk after it.

"Does he not know that dogs cannot climb trees?" Julia asked her sister.

Hannah laughed. "Fluff does not know that he is a dog," she replied.

They continued through the woods, enjoying the cool pine-scented air, watching for squirrels and chipmunks. Joseph chased after Fluff, running and jumping and barking as if he, too, were a dog.

Robert shifted the basket from hand to hand, complaining about its weight. Brandon picked up stones and threw them on the path.

"Does Father know we are having a picnic in the woods?" he asked Julia.

"I wanted to tell him," she replied, brushing a white burr from the front of her long gingham skirt. "But he was upstairs in Mother's room. She was having another one of her spells, I am afraid."

"Mother and her spells," Hannah said, rolling her eyes.

"Here is a nice clearing," Robert said happily. A circle of tall grass appeared like an oasis among the trees. "Can we have our lunch here?"

"Very well," Julia agreed brightly. "This shall do fine."

"Freedom!" Robert cried, setting the basket down, then stretching his arms.

Julia and Hannah spread a red wool blanket over the grass. Fluff immediately leapt onto the blanket, tracking dirt and leaves over it. Hannah brushed the little dog away. Julia opened the lid of the basket and began to pull items from it and set them down on the blanket.

"Look! Is that a deer?" Robert cried.

"Where?" Joseph spun around wildly, searching all directions at once.

"Follow me," Robert instructed his brothers. "But keep silent. Let's track him!"

The boys headed off at a run toward the trees. "Do not go far!" Julia called after them. "It is almost lunchtime!"

"Mmmmm. Those little pies look good," Hannah told her sister, dropping to her knees on the blanket. "I am suddenly starving."

"Fresh air makes me hungry, too," Julia replied. "Let's see . . . Lucy packed a little meat pie for each of us. And there are raisin cookies and a jug of fresh lemon water." She handed a meat pie to her sister. "Let's eat. We need not wait for the boys."

Hannah raised the small doughy pie to her mouth and was about to take a bite when Fluff leapt into her lap. "Oh!" she cried out, startled.

The dog raised himself on his hind legs and sniffed the pie in Hannah's hand noisily.

"You little beggar!" Hannah cried, laughing. "Down, down! Get off me, and I shall give you a taste!"

Ignoring her, Fluff leapt high, trying to get his teeth on the meat pie.

"Here. Here is a piece for you," Hannah said, using one hand to shove the dog off her lap. She broke off a tiny wedge of pie and held it out to Fluff.

The dog yipped and slurped it up eagerly, licking Hannah's hand clean. "Stop! Stop! You're *tickling* me!" she cried, laughing. "What a scratchy tongue you have, doggy!"

"You *do* spoil that dog," Julia grumbled good-naturedly.

Hannah gave Fluff another piece of the pie.

"Where are the boys?" Julia asked. She climbed to her feet, shielding her eyes with one hand, and searched the woods for them.

"I hope they have not wandered far," Hannah

said, following her sister's gaze. "Robert has no sense of direction at all. He can get lost inside the house!"

Hearing a strange sound, Hannah turned back to Fluff.

To her surprise, the dog was whimpering loudly, his head lowered, his tail tucked tightly between his legs.

As Hannah watched in alarm, the dog's entire body began to convulse. Fluff coughed, then his stomach heaved, and he began to vomit, his legs trembling, his entire body quivering.

Then all at once the dog crumpled to the blanket, dropped onto his side, and was still.

"Fluff!" Hannah cried. "Fluff! Fluff! Oh, Julia— what has happened?"

Chapter
16

Hannah carefully lifted the dog from a puddle of dark vomit and held him tightly against the front of her dress. "He's dead," she muttered.

"No!" Julia cried in horror. "Hannah, he *cannot* be! He—" Tears formed in the corners of Julia's gray eyes.

"Poor Fluff. Poor Fluff. Poor Fluff," Hannah repeated quietly, still hugging the dead animal to her.

"No. I do not believe it!" Julia cried, shaking her head. "The dog was perfectly fine until— until—"

Both girls had the idea at the same time.

"The meat pies!" Hannah cried. Her eyes widened in horror, and she gaped at her sister. "Julia, did you—?"

Julia lowered her eyes to the pie beside her on the blanket. "No. I did not touch mine. You?"

Hannah shook her head. "Only Fluff. He was the only one to eat. And now the poor dog is dead."

"Poisoned," Julia muttered.

Hannah gasped. *"What* did you say, sister?"

"Poisoned," Julia repeated the word as she wiped the tears from her eyes. "Lucy. She poisoned the pies. She *had* to."

"No!" Hannah cried, lowering the dog to the blanket, her features set in horror. "You don't think—"

"Lucy," her sister repeated, shaking her head. "She almost murdered us all."

Hannah swallowed hard, her heart thudding wildly against her chest. She climbed quickly to her feet, her expression frightened. "Where are the boys?" she asked, searching the woods. "Julia, go fetch the boys and bring them home. I shall run to tell Father. He must know what Lucy has done—at once!"

As Hannah ran through the woods toward the house, tears rolled down her cheeks.

Poor Fluff, she thought. That poor, innocent dog. He looked so frightened, so confused.

Poisoned.

Poisoned by that villainous maid.

If only Hannah had told her father her suspicions about Lucy after finding the shard of glass in her shoe. Then Fluff would still be alive.

I'll tell Father everything now, Hannah told

herself. And the maid will be gone before—before she can kill again.

The back of the rambling Fear mansion came into view. Hannah slowed a little as she passed the burial plot. A closed pine coffin had been set down at the edge of the fresh grave.

Jenkins must be inside it, Hannah realized. The funeral will be held in a few moments.

Thinking of Fluff, a loud sob escaped her throat. Hannah turned away from the narrow coffin and ran the rest of the way to the house.

She burst through the door to the back pantry. "Father! Father! Are you downstairs?" she called breathlessly.

No reply.

In the kitchen bright sunlight streamed across the floor from the back window.

"Father? Father?"

No one there.

Frantically, Hannah started toward the hallway.

But a black-uniformed figure moved quickly to block her path.

"Lucy!"

Chapter
17

The sunlight washed over Lucy as she stepped toward Hannah. Her orange hair was secured tightly in a bun. Her eyes locked on Hannah's.

"Lucy—why did you *poison* us?" Hannah blurted out, panting for breath. "Why?"

"What?" Lucy's mouth dropped open.

"Do not play innocent!" Hannah cried angrily. "Why did you poison our lunch?"

"I have no idea what you are talking about, miss," Lucy replied, turning up her sharp nose.

"You murdered my dog!" Hannah shrieked.

"What is all the noise in here?" Mrs. MacKenzie bustled in from the hallway. "Hannah, what is the matter?" the housekeeper asked with concern.

"Lucy tried to poison us!" Hannah cried, pointing at the maid, who took another step back. "She poisoned the meat pies!"

"What?" Mrs. MacKenzie narrowed her eyes at Hannah. "What are you saying about meat pies? The meat pies for your picnic?"

"Yes," Hannah cried. "They were poisoned! Lucy has been trying to harm us since she arrived. And today—"

"No!" Lucy screamed, interrupting. "No! You are telling lies, miss!"

Ignoring her protests, Hannah turned to Mrs. MacKenzie. "I must get my father. He must know at once. Lucy poisoned the pies!"

"No, she did not," Mrs. MacKenzie said firmly, placing her hands on the sides of her long apron.

"What?" Hannah had started to the door but stopped short.

"As I am a witness, Lucy did *not* poison the pies," Mrs. MacKenzie repeated, frowning, her round cheeks a bright pink. "Lucy had nothing to do with your lunch, Miss Hannah. Your sister Julia prepared the lunch."

Hannah felt dazed. The room suddenly tilted. The bright sunlight washing over her made everything go white. "Julia?"

"Miss Julia made the pies," Mrs. MacKenzie insisted. "Lucy asked if Julia needed help. But Miss Julia ordered Lucy to stay out of the kitchen."

"Julia?" Hannah gasped weakly. "No. Please. Not Julia. Not Julia."

"Miss Hannah, are you feeling ill?" Mrs. Mac-Kenzie demanded, tugging on the sides of her apron. "Perhaps I should summon your father?"

But Hannah was already running through the back pantry and out the door.

Her heart pounding, her head spinning from what she had just learned, she ran past the flower garden and across the lawn. She saw her brothers first, coming out of the woods. Their faces were drawn. Julia must have told them about Fluff. The boys nodded solemnly at Hannah, then continued on in silence toward the house.

Julia appeared next. As she stepped out of the woods, she stopped a few yards from Jenkins's coffin.

She was carrying the picnic basket, but set it down when she saw Hannah hurrying toward her. "Hannah, did you find Father? Did you tell him about Lucy?"

Panting hard, struggling to catch her breath, Hannah stared intently at her sister, studying her face, searching for the truth in Julia's small gray eyes.

"Julia—it was *you!*" Hannah finally managed to choke out.

As she stared back at Hannah, Julia's eyes turned cold. She nodded.

"*You* tried to poison me," Hannah accused, her voice just above a whisper.

Julia didn't deny it. She stared back, emotionless, her expression a blank.

"Why, Julia?" Hannah demanded. "Why?"

"I hate you, Hannah," Julia replied quietly, calmly. "I want you to die."

"But why? Why? Why?" Hannah shrieked. She realized she was more horrified by Julia's coldness than by her action.

"Why should *you* be the hostess?" Julia demanded, her black curls falling forward. She made no attempt to push them back. "Why should I not be the pretty one? The charming one? Why should *I* not be Father's favorite? Why should I not take Mother's place? I am the oldest—and the smartest. And— and—"

Her normally pale face was scarlet now. Her eyes burned into Hannah's. Her shoulders trembled. Julia's hands were balled into tight, angry fists at her sides.

Hannah shrank back, suddenly frightened. "Julia, you—*you* put the snake in my bed! *You* put the glass in my shoe. *You*—" Hannah's terrified voice caught in her throat.

Julia didn't deny it. "I wanted you to be scared. I wanted you to bleed. I want you to *die!*"

With a furious cry Julia attacked Hannah, leaping onto her, wrapping her hands around Hannah's throat.

Startled, caught completely off guard, Hannah stumbled and fell backward. She landed hard on her elbows and cried out from the pain.

Julia landed on top of her, her hands still at Hannah's throat.

Crying and groaning, the two girls wrestled on the ground—until Hannah broke free, climbed to her feet, and started to run.

But Julia was faster and tackled her sister hard from behind.

Hannah landed on her stomach on top of the pine coffin. She groaned and tried to pull herself up.

But Julia was on top of her again, pressing her down onto the hard coffin. And again Julia's hands wrapped around Hannah's throat.

"Die! Die! Die!" Julia shrieked at the top of her lungs as her hands tightened viciously around Hannah's throat.

Hannah struggled to roll free, to get off the coffin.

But Julia held tight as she choked off Hannah's air.

Chapter
18

========

Hannah gasped for breath, thrashing her arms frantically, trying to grab Julia, to push her away.

But Julia was too strong, too determined.

Hannah felt herself weaken, felt her muscles go slack, felt her body surrender.

Everything went bright red. Blood red. Then bright white. Hannah felt herself sinking, sinking into the white nothingness.

And then—miraculously—Julia's hands slipped away from Hannah's throat.

Hannah stared up at the white, white sky. Color returned slowly.

She took a short breath. Then another. The air made a whistling sound as it entered her lungs.

Julia thinks I am dead, Hannah realized. She believes she has murdered me. That is why she has released my throat.

Hannah sucked in another breath of air.

A sound in the woods behind them caused Julia to turn her back. Was there someone there? Had someone seen them?

No, it was only a deer scurrying in the underbrush. Julia bent over, hands on her knees, panting loudly.

She thinks she has murdered me.

The words repeated in Hannah's mind, turning her fear to anger. With a burst of strength she rolled off the coffin and landed on her feet.

Hannah stood unsteadily, the ground swaying beneath her.

"You—you're alive?" Julia cried breathlessly, spinning around, her eyes wide. She recovered quickly and lunged at Hannah.

Hannah grabbed the first thing she saw—the heavy iron shovel that had been used to dig Jenkins's grave.

As Julia leapt at her, Hannah cried out and swung the shovel.

It made a metallic *clang* as it slammed against Julia's head.

Julia's eyes bulged wide. Then they rolled up in her head as she dropped to her knees. Blood spurted from her nose, flowed down her chin. Finally she dropped facedown into the grass.

Hannah stared in horror, shaking all over, the

heavy shovel still gripped tightly in both her hands. She watched the bright blood, Julia's blood, puddle on the grass.

I have killed her, she realized. *I have killed Julia.*

The shovel fell at Hannah's feet. She wrapped her arms around herself, trying to stop her body from trembling.

Now what?

She couldn't think clearly. Everything kept turning red, then white. Flashing crazily in front of her. The clouds overhead appeared to race. The sun dipped, then rose again.

Crazy. All too crazy.

Julia is dead.

Now what?

Before Hannah even realized what she was doing, she had pulled open the pine lid of the gardener's coffin. The stale aroma of his corpse floated up to greet her.

The old man's purple face stared blankly up at her. The eyes had sunk deep into Jenkins's skull. The lips were pulled tight in a hideous death grin.

Sobbing loudly, struggling to hold back her disgust, Hannah frantically grabbed her sister's body under the arms and pulled it to the coffin. Lifted. Lifted Julia's body, so heavy in death.

Shoved it into the coffin. On top of the rotting gardener.

Shoved it. Sobbing. Trembling. Shoved it. Shoved it in.

One arm draped itself over the side of the coffin. Hannah grabbed the arm with both hands and bent it into the coffin.

And slammed the lid shut. And clasped it.

And ran blindly to the woods to vomit. To spew up the horror. The horror of having killed her only sister.

Her only sister, who had hated Hannah enough to try to murder *her*.

Choking and sobbing, Hannah clung to the cool trunk of a tree. And waited for her mind to clear, for the ground to stop swaying, for the lights to stop flashing in her head.

Hannah was still at the edge of the woods, still clinging to the solid tree trunk, when the small party of mourners gathered around the freshly dug grave to bury Jenkins.

Her cheek pressed against the smooth bark, Hannah watched the dark-coated minister, Bible in hand, say a few words over the coffin. The mourners, servants from the house and a few people from the village, bowed their heads as the minister spoke.

Then Hannah saw the strongest of the men step forward to lift the coffin into the grave. They struggled for a moment, surprised by the weight of it. Then, working silently together, they lowered the box into the ground and covered it with dirt, using the same shovel Hannah had used to kill Julia.

Julia is in the ground now, Hannah thought,

watching the members of the small funeral party walking slowly toward the house. Julia is in the ground with Jenkins.

Hannah stayed in the woods a long while. When the sun began to lower itself behind the trees and the air grew evening cool, she wiped the tearstains from her cheeks. Then she straightened her dress and slowly walked back to the house.

"Where is Julia?" Simon asked.

Hannah pretended not to hear the question. She was slumped in a chair in a corner of the sitting room, watching Brandon and Joseph toss a small ball back and forth in front of the fire.

"Has anyone seen Julia?" Simon repeated impatiently from the doorway, his eyes on Hannah.

"I have not seen her, Father. Not since our picnic in the woods behind the house," Brandon replied, bouncing the ball gently to his little brother.

"Maybe she is still outside," Joseph said, missing the ball and scrambling after it.

"Can you two not find a better indoor activity?" Simon scolded sharply. He disappeared before the boys could reply.

Hannah shivered in spite of the heat that filled the room from the glowing fireplace. She stared at the boys but didn't really see them. Instead she saw the pine box. She saw Julia's arm hanging over the side of it. Then she saw the heavy pine box being lowered into the ground.

"Julia? Julia, are you upstairs?" Hannah heard her father shout up the stairs.

No. Julia is not upstairs, Hannah thought dully. Julia is not in the house, Father. Julia is in the ground.

"Julia? Where is Julia?" She heard her father calling. "Has anyone seen Julia?"

Chapter
19

================

Muttering to himself, Simon Fear pulled his cloak around himself as he stepped into the evening darkness. Having searched the entire house for his daughter, he decided to try the garden.

Sometimes Julia would completely lose track of the time, and Simon would find her on a bench in the garden, dreamily poring over a book of romantic poetry.

A pale crescent moon rose above the woods at the end of the back lawn. The sky was still a royal evening blue. A cool wind picked up and blew against Simon as he crossed the yard.

"Julia? Are you out here?" The wind threw his voice back to him. He pulled the cloak tighter.

The roses on the tall trellises bobbed in the gusting breeze. The wind howled through the trees.

Or *was* it the wind?

Simon stopped and stood perfectly still, holding his cloak in place, his head tilted as he listened intently.

What was that horrible howl? That pained cry?

Simon took a few steps toward the frightening sound. He stood near the family burial plot, his eyes narrowed, listening.

There it was again.

A frightening shriek. Like the cry of a trapped animal.

Another shriek, high-pitched. A moan.

Simon turned toward the gardening sheds at the fence. Has a wild animal gotten itself trapped in one of the sheds? he wondered.

Another mournful howl.

No. The sound was too close.

So nearby.

Simon grasped his cloak as another shrill cry rose on a gust of wind.

He stared down at the ground. It seemed as if the sound was at his feet.

"But that's impossible!" he cried.

And then he realized that he was standing beside a freshly dug grave, the dark earth still mounded loose over the coffin.

Mr. Jenkins's grave.

Another pitiful cry, a desperate animal shriek.

From the ground. From the grave.

Someone crying out from the new grave.

A girl.

Julia!

"No!" Simon uttered, terror choking him.

Before he realized what he was doing, he had picked up the shovel and begun digging into the earth.

His heart pounding, Simon frantically shoveled, the blade cutting easily into the soft dirt. Working feverishly, he tossed the dirt over his shoulder, digging down, down—until finally, when he felt his chest was about to burst, the shovel hit something solid. The lid of the coffin.

"Yes!" Simon cried and began digging wildly, scraping and shoving the dirt out of the hole.

So close! So close!

"I'm coming!" he screamed in a panic-filled voice he didn't recognize. "I'm coming! I'm coming!"

He didn't try to lift the coffin. Instead he tossed the shovel aside and leapt down into the hole.

With trembling hands he lifted the latch. Then, gasping loudly, his heart thudding against his chest, he pulled up the coffin lid.

Chapter
20

"Julia!"

Simon cried out when he saw his daughter sprawled on top of the gardener's corpse.

Her black hair had fallen over her face. He brushed it back gently, his hand trembling, loud sobs escaping his throat.

Dead. She was dead.

So pale. Her face was locked in a grimace of terror, her lifeless eyes wide. Dried blood was caked over her nose and chin.

"Noooooooo!" The howl erupted from Simon. It echoed against the dark walls of the grave he had opened.

He gaped in horror at his daughter. Her fingernails were torn and bloodied. Simon saw long scratch marks along the inside of the coffin lid.

Buried alive, he realized. *Julia was buried alive.*

The wind howled above him. He gazed up at the sliver of pale moon. He couldn't bear to look at her any longer.

"Who?" he cried, scrambling out of the hole, scrabbling over the soft dirt, his arms thrashing wildly. "Who did this? Who?"

Back up on solid ground, he staggered toward the house. "Who did this? Who murdered my daughter?"

He tossed the cloak to the ground and began to run.

The house loomed ahead, a dark blur. The whole world had become a dark blur.

Moments later he stood in the kitchen, struggling to catch his breath, struggling to stop the painful pounding of his heart.

"Mrs. MacKenzie! Mrs. MacKenzie!" he screamed frantically. Where was she? Where was everyone?

He grabbed on to a sideboard to keep himself from collapsing.

Something near his hand caught his attention.

A long sheet of paper with scribbled words down one side. Scribbled names.

The servant's list.

The newly written name at the bottom of the list, the ink still dark and fresh.

LUCY GOODE.

"Nooooooooooooo!" A wild animal howl erupted from deep inside him.

"Not a Goode! Not a Goode in my house!"

117

Simon truly believed the Goodes had vanished from the earth. He believed he had killed the last of them—Frank Goode—back in Wickham when he was still a boy.

He believed that the curse had ended that long-ago day. That no member of the Goode family could ever threaten the Fears again.

And now here was a Goode hiding in his own household, carrying on the evil of the Goodes against the Fears—*murdering his Julia!*

"Nooooooo!" Simon grasped the silver pendant tightly in one hand. He felt its warmth, felt its power.

His rage carried him into the front parlor.

He picked out a sword from the new collection of war relics. He waved it high. It gleamed in the light from the gas lamps.

He followed the sword's gleam.

Running frantically, bellowing his rage, Simon followed the glow of the sword through the house.

I will find her. I will find Lucy Goode!

I will put an end to the evil she has brought to my house, to my family!

"Simon! What are you *doing!* Simon!"

Was that Angelica calling to him from the stairway?

He did not slow down. He followed the glowing sword. Glowing like a torch now. Glowing with the heat of his vengeance.

"Simon—stop!"

Angelica sounded so far away.

I will find her. I will find the maid—

There she stood!

A bright blurred figure walking toward him, beyond the blinding glow of the sword blade.

Yes! He had found her!

Yes!

The maid. The Goode. A Goode walking in his very own hallway.

"Simon—*stop!*" Angelica called.

But Simon could not stop.

He lowered the gleaming sword.

The girl shrieked and threw her hands up in terror.

He had her. He had her now.

The sword glowed so brightly, so brightly he could see only its light.

"Simon—*stop! Stop!*" Angelica screamed.

But Simon plunged the sword deep into the maid's chest.

Chapter
21

The light shimmered around Simon, blinding white light.

As he thrust the sword into Lucy Goode and she uttered a choking gasp of pain, the light grew even brighter.

A small round dark spot formed in the center of the light. The spot grew, spreading its darkness.

It took Simon a while to realize that the spot was blood, blood staining the front of the girl's dress.

Darker, darker. The spot expanded until it blocked out the light.

And as the darkness grew and the shimmering light faded, Simon's vision was restored. He could see clearly once again.

Still holding the long ebony handle of the sword,

staring at the blood as it stained the dress, Simon could see. Could see that he hadn't stabbed Lucy Goode.

He had thrust the sword deep into his own daughter's chest.

"Simon! Simon!" Angelica's shrill cries repeated in his ears, shutting out all other sounds, shutting out his own horrified thoughts. "Simon! Simon! Simon!"

Then Hannah fell forward and slumped into her father's arms, as his sword clanged heavily to the floor.

Warm blood poured over Simon's evening shirt. Hannah's blood.

She uttered a soft moan. Her lips continued to move after all sound had died.

All sound except Angelica's shrill chant: "Simon! Simon! Simon!"

Hannah died in Simon's arms, her head lying heavily against his shoulder, her soft blond hair brushing his cheek, falling over his shoulder.

Hannah dead. Julia dead.

Angelica shrieked, her eyes shut tight, pulling frantically at her long black hair.

Robert held his brothers, turning them away from the hideous scene before them.

Mrs. MacKenzie sobbed against the wall, burying her face in her apron.

"I—I thought it was Lucy Goode," Simon sputtered.

"Lucy Goode resigned this afternoon," Mrs.

MacKenzie replied through her sobs. "She could not bear Miss Hannah's accusations. She packed her bag and departed."

With a quiet shudder Simon held his lifeless daughter. As he struggled to keep her on her feet, they appeared to be dancing, a strange, sad, awkward last dance.

Hannah is gone, he realized. Julia is gone. The wonderful part of my life is over.

"Simon! Simon! Simon!" Angelica chanted.

"I tried to hide from it, Angelica," Simon sobbed. "I tried to pretend it no longer existed. But the curse that follows the Fear family has found us all today."

"Simon! Simon! Simon!" Angelica shrieked behind him. "Simon! Simon! Simon!"

Simon Fear knew that her cries would haunt him for the rest of his life.

PART THREE

Shadyside Village
1900

Chapter
22

On a gloomy fall day a young man stepped off the westbound train onto the narrow concrete platform of the Shadyside train station. He was a good-looking boy of eighteen, with slicked-down brown hair, lively brown eyes, and a friendly, open face.

He quickly glanced down the main street of the small town. Shadyside appeared to be prosperous and pleasant with low brick buildings behind shady trees. Then he hailed a carriage with a cheerful cry. "Cabbie! Cabbie!"

The driver, a shriveled old man with white whiskers and long white sideburns beneath a worn blue cap, stopped the horses and hopped down to help the young man with his suitcase.

"I can handle it, driver," the young man said,

offering his friendly smile. "I have but one bag, as you can see."

"And where do you come from?" the cabbie asked, eyeing the boy suspiciously.

"Boston" was the reply. "My name is Daniel. Daniel Fear. And I have come to visit my grandparents."

The old driver's eyes narrowed in surprise. "Daniel Fear, did you say? And you have come to visit Simon Fear and his wife?"

"They are my grandparents. I have never met them," Daniel admitted. He hoisted his bag onto the luggage compartment at the back of the carriage. One of the two horses whinnied. The carriage rocked back and forth.

"My name is McGuire," the cabbie said, touching his cap. "I have been driving this rig in Shadyside Village for a lot longer than you have been alive, son. And you are the first visitor I have ever taken to the Fear mansion."

"Strange," Daniel replied uncertainly.

"Strange indeed," McGuire said, shaking his head. "That house has been dark and closed up ever since the two daughters died. That was some thirty-five years ago, I believe."

"Simon's daughters?" Daniel asked, surprised. "You mean that I had aunts?"

The cabbie nodded. "Who might your father be, son?"

"Joseph Fear," Daniel told him.

"Ah, yes, Joseph," McGuire said, removing his cap to scratch his head. "I remember him well.

Good-looking boy. I remember they sent him away to school. A couple of years after the . . . uh . . . after the tragedy with the two girls. Joseph never returned home."

"Yes. We live in Boston now," Daniel said. "None of us has ever been back to Shadyside. My father is a very quiet man, a private man. He never told us much about our family. I did not even know I *had* grandparents here until word came about my grandfather's seventy-fifth birthday."

"So Simon Fear is to be seventy-five," McGuire muttered, rubbing his chin.

"Yes," Daniel replied. "My grandfather wrote a letter and asked to see me. So . . . here I am."

The old cabbie muttered something that Daniel couldn't hear. Then he turned and, with a loud groan, hoisted himself up to the driver's seat. Daniel watched McGuire take the reins, then climbed inside the small carriage, pulling the door closed beside him.

Staring out the dusty window, Daniel watched the small town roll by. The town center with its offices and shops gave way to rows of small cottages, then farm fields, then tangled woods. The overcast sky made everything appear dark and unwelcoming.

Suddenly Daniel heard McGuire shout for the horses to *whoa,* and the carriage bounced to an abrupt stop. Daniel peered out at a tall brass gate. The gate was tarnished.

"Here we are, son," McGuire called down. "The Fear mansion."

Daniel opened the carriage door and leaned out. "Can you not take me up the driveway?"

His question was greeted by a long silence. Finally the old man called down gruffly, "This is as far as I go. Few people would wish to come as near as this to Simon Fear's mansion."

Daniel climbed down and removed his bag. He handed up two coins to the driver, who stared straight ahead, refusing to look at the mansion. Then with a curt "Good luck, son," McGuire whipped the horses, and the carriage sped away.

Daniel pushed open the heavy gate and stepped onto the long dirt driveway that led up to the house. "Oh!" The sight of the enormous mansion looming against the charcoal gray sky made Daniel stop and cry out.

Tall weeds choked the lawn. Shrubs and hedges had grown wild. A fallen tree limb lay across a barren, neglected flowerbed.

The house, a ramshackle, dark fortress, stretched behind a thick veil of bent trees. All of the windows were shuttered. No welcoming light greeted Daniel as he trudged up the driveway. No light escaped from the house at all.

So *this* is where Father grew up! he thought in amazement. What a dreary, frightening old place. No *wonder* Father never talks about his childhood.

Dead, brown leaves rustled at Daniel's feet as he stepped up to the double front door and lifted the heavy brass knocker. He could hear the bang of the knocker echoing inside the house.

He waited, listening. He knocked again.

Finally the heavy door creaked open.

A stooped, white-haired old woman poked her head out and stared up at him suspiciously. She wore a stained white apron over a black dress. One of her eyes had glazed over. It was solid gray. The other eye squinted hard at him.

Frowning, she muttered something that Daniel couldn't hear.

"I beg your pardon?" he asked, leaning closer.

"Stay away!" the old woman rasped. *"Stay away from here!"*

Chapter
23

Startled, Daniel stared back at the old woman. "I am Daniel Fear," he said finally. "I believe my grandfather is expecting me."

The old woman sighed but didn't reply. She squinted up at him for a long time with her one good eye. Then she beckoned him inside, gesturing with a bony, gnarled finger.

"I am Mrs. MacKenzie, the housekeeper," she told him, leaning on a white cane as she led him through a long, dark hallway. "I am housekeeper, maid, valet, and butler," she added with some bitterness. "The only servant who stayed."

Daniel followed her in silence, carrying his bag. As they made their way through narrow, dark hallways, he tried to peer into the rooms they passed. They all seemed to be dark and shuttered, the furniture covered with sheets.

"My father did not tell me the house was so large," Daniel said, his voice echoing in the empty hall.

"Your father got away . . ." Mrs. MacKenzie answered mysteriously.

They continued through the dark, gloomy house in silence. The only sounds Daniel heard were the scraping of his boots on the threadbare carpet and the *tap-tap-tap* of the old housekeeper's white cane as she walked.

At the end of a twisting hallway Daniel saw a flicker of orange light from a corner room. "Your grandparents are in there," Mrs. MacKenzie said softly, pointing. She turned, leaving him in the hall, and disappeared around a corner, her cane tapping its insistent rhythm.

Is the old woman completely mad? Daniel wondered. Or just unfriendly?

He took a deep breath and reluctantly approached the doorway. He saw a low fire crackling in a wide stone fireplace. Setting down his suitcase, Daniel stepped into the room.

His grandmother caught his eye first. Angelica was stretched out on a purple velvet chaise longue beside the fire. She wore an elegant black dress with a white lace collar.

She smiled at Daniel as he approached, but made no attempt to stand up. As she smiled, Daniel saw that her skin was delicate and translucent and tight against the bone, making her face resemble that of a grinning skull. Her hair fell loosely down her back. It was as white as snow.

"Grandmother Angelica," Daniel said with a slight bow. He reached for her hand, but she didn't offer it.

"Put another log on the fire, boy," Angelica ordered.

"I beg your pardon?" Daniel had expected a warmer greeting from his grandmother.

"Do not dawdle. Do as I say," Angelica insisted coldly, waving a slender white hand toward the fire. "Another log on the fire, boy."

Daniel hesitated, then hurried to the fireplace to do her bidding. He could find no logs in the wood basket, so he piled on several sticks of kindling.

Then, wiping his hands, he turned back to his grandmother. "I am so pleased to meet you," he said, smiling sincerely.

"You may go now," Angelica replied curtly. Before the startled Daniel could reply, she started to scream: *"Did you not hear me? Go! Go! Go!"*

Daniel gaped at her, trying to decide what to say or do.

"Pay no attention to her," a high-pitched voice wheezed from behind him.

Daniel wheeled around and saw a nearly bald old man hunched over in a wooden wheelchair. He had a thin brown blanket tucked over his legs. His face was yellow and sickly in the flickering firelight. He stared at Daniel through square-shaped spectacles with his dark eyes, eyes like tiny black buttons.

"Grandfather!" Daniel declared.

Simon Fear wheeled himself closer, both hands pushing at the large wooden wheelchair wheels. "Pay no attention to Angelica. She is mad! Mad as a loon!" He cackled as if he had made a joke.

Daniel glanced back at Angelica, who lay staring at the fire.

"Grandfather Simon, I am pleased to meet you," Daniel said, turning back to the frail old man.

Simon extended a slender, spotted hand to his grandson. Daniel reached down to shake hands. He almost cried out. Simon's hand was unearthly cold!

"Joseph's boy," Simon muttered, refusing to let go of Daniel's hand. Behind the eyeglasses the tiny black sparrow eyes had locked on Daniel's face as if trying to memorize every detail. "Yes, yes. I see Joseph in you," he said and then coughed for several seconds, allowing Daniel the opportunity to remove his hand from the icy grip.

"My father sends his love," Daniel said stiffly.

"Love? What is love?" Angelica chimed in from behind him. "What is love? I would really like to know."

"Joseph has no love for us," Simon said darkly, wiping saliva from his colorless lips with the back of his hand.

"I beg your pardon?" Daniel exclaimed.

"My son Joseph abandoned us. I tried to make him understand that we Fears have no choice but to stick together, to band together, to hide together against our enemies. But Joseph chose to disobey me."

The light seemed to fade from Simon's eyes. He lowered his head. For a moment Daniel thought that his grandfather had fallen asleep.

"Put another log on the fire!" Angelica ordered impatiently. "Another log, if you please! Why must it always be so cold in here?"

"There do not seem to be any more logs," Daniel told his grandmother.

An icy hand grabbed his wrist. Simon held him with surprising strength. "I told you to ignore her!" he snapped.

Daniel tried to pull free. The cold from Simon's hand seemed to sweep right through Daniel's entire body. "Grandfather—"

"You cannot hide from your blood!" Simon declared loudly, staring up at Daniel, tightening his cold grip on his grandson's wrist. "I told Joseph that when he was just a boy. You cannot hide from your blood and your fate."

"Yes, Grandfather," Daniel stammered, trying to be polite.

"His brothers Robert and Brandon stayed," Simon said. "But now they're gone too."

"I never met my uncles," Daniel replied softly.

"Now you are here, Daniel," Simon said, smiling up at him, a frightening smile that sent shivers up Daniel's spine. "Now you are here to carry on my work."

Daniel swallowed hard. "Your work? I—I came to celebrate your birthday, Grandfather. I—"

Simon ignored him. He had both hands up behind his collar, struggling to remove something from around his neck. Finally he succeeded. With another frightening smile he tucked an object into Daniel's hand.

Daniel took a step back toward the fireplace and examined his grandfather's gift. To his surprise it was a piece of silver jewelry. Disk shaped, it was held by three silver claws, like birds' feet. On the disk were four blue jewels that sparkled brightly in the firelight.

What a strange gift, Daniel thought. He turned the pendant over. On the back he found Latin words inscribed: DOMINATIO PER MALUM.

"What do these words mean, Grandfather?" Daniel asked, studying the strange silver pendant.

"Power through evil!" Simon bellowed. His loud cry caused him to cough and wheeze.

Daniel studied the strange pendant, turning it over in his hands.

"Put it on," Simon instructed him. "Wear it always. It has been in the Fear family since our days in the Old Country."

Daniel obediently slipped the silver chain around his neck.

He tucked the pendant under his dress shirt.

And as the warm disk settled against his chest, he felt a surge of heat—and the entire room burst into flame!

Chapter
24

Daniel saw flames before him—the bright image of flames leaping tall into a black sky. A momentary image, a vision, lasting a second or two.

In the flames he saw a girl, a young girl, pretty and blond, twisting in the fire, twisting in agony.

The image disappeared. The girl and the flames vanished instantly.

The pendant still felt warm against his chest.

Simon smiled knowingly up at his grandson.

The strange three-clawed pendant has powers, Daniel realized, feeling fear and curiosity at once.

Daniel heard a tapping sound behind him. He turned to see Mrs. MacKenzie enter the room, bent over her cane, an unpleasant frown on her withered face.

"I have come to take the young gentleman to his room," she announced coldly, glaring at Simon with her one good eye.

Simon didn't reply. He nodded. His eyes closed.

"Put another log on the fire, boy," Angelica ordered. "I'm cold—so cold!"

Mrs. MacKenzie grunted her disapproval of her mistress. Feeling awkward and confused, Daniel picked up his bag and followed the old housekeeper out of the room.

Tapping her cane against the thin carpets, she led him through a twisting maze of dark halls. Then up creaking stairs to a large bedroom on the second floor.

Daniel followed her in. The room was cold. The small fire in the fireplace offered little heat. Mrs. MacKenzie made her way to the window and pulled the shutters open to allow some light in. But the windows were caked with soot.

She offered Daniel a helpless shrug, then hurried from the room, her cane tapping in front of her.

Daniel slumped onto the bed, shivering. "Why have I come here?" he asked himself out loud.

Shaking his head unhappily, he removed his pocket watch and studied it. Hours to go before dinner. And Simon's birthday party is several weeks away.

What will I do here? How will I spend the time?

Staring into the small, useless fire, Daniel wished he had never come.

* * *

Dinner was solitary and silent. Simon and Angelica were nowhere to be seen. Mrs. MacKenzie served Daniel his dinner at one end of the long dining room table. He had little appetite but forced himself to eat.

The next day he made his way into town and strolled around Shadyside Village, delighted to be out of the stale air and gloomy surroundings of the Fear mansion.

He found the town square pretty and pleasant. People smiled at him as he passed. Daniel was so good-looking and friendly, he often drew smiles from strangers.

A crowd of villagers had gathered at the edge of the square to admire a shiny new motorcar, one of the few "horseless carriages" that Daniel had seen in Boston. Eagerly he strolled over to see it. A strange-looking four-wheeled contraption of glass and painted metal.

A red-faced man in his shirtsleeves was straining hard, turning a metal crank at the front of the machine, trying to start it up. But in spite of the enthusiastic support of the crowd, the engine refused to sputter to life.

Chuckling to himself, Daniel stepped away and realized he was quite thirsty, probably from the dust that floated up from Shadyside's unpaved streets.

A small white-fronted general store on the corner caught his eye, and he made his way toward it, thinking of a cold drink.

As he pulled open the door, the aroma of fresh-brewed coffee greeted his nostrils. He closed the door behind him. Then, stepping past a large wooden pickle barrel and several burlap bags of flour and sugar, he stopped at the long wooden counter at the back of the store.

A young woman dressed in a silky yellow high-collared blouse and long maroon skirt had her back to him. She was reaching up to arrange canisters on a shelf on the wall.

Daniel cleared his throat impatiently.

She turned and smiled, surprised to see a stranger in the store.

And Daniel fell in love.

She is the most beautiful girl I have ever seen, Daniel thought, feeling dazed.

She appeared to be about his age with long dark hair that fell to her shoulders, creamy pale skin, and green eyes that gleamed in the light from the store window.

Her smile, the most beautiful smile Daniel had ever seen, faded. "Are you staring at me?" she demanded. Her voice was lower, throatier than he had expected.

"Yes," he replied. He couldn't think of any other reply.

Speechless. I'm speechless, he thought. Maybe coming to Shadyside was not such a bad idea after all.

He suddenly realized she was gazing at him with

concern, her broad forehead wrinkling above the beautiful green eyes.

He blinked. Felt himself blushing.

"Are you feeling well?" she asked, hanging back from the counter.

"I—I apologize," Daniel managed to stammer. "I—I am thirsty. So—"

"Would you like coffee? Or perhaps some some apple cider?" she suggested, her smile returning. "It is very fresh."

Daniel adjusted the starched collar of his shirt. It suddenly felt very tight. "Yes. Thank you. Cider would be wonderful."

"Well, it *is* good. I do not know if it is wonderful," she replied dryly. With a sweep of her long skirt she made her way around the counter, carrying a tin cup toward the cider barrel across the aisle.

She walks so gracefully, Daniel thought, following her with his eyes. Like a poem. He suddenly wished he knew poetry.

She handed him the cup filled with cider. He took a sip. "Very good." He licked his lips. He raised his eyes to hers and realized that *she* was now staring at *him*.

She glanced away shyly. "Are you new in town?"

Daniel told her he was. "Can you tell me of some interesting places I should see?"

She laughed. "Interesting? In *Shadyside?*"

He laughed with her. He liked her sense of humor. And he liked the way her chin trembled when she laughed. And he liked her low, velvety voice.

"Surely there must be something worth seeing," he protested.

She narrowed her green eyes as she thought. "I am sorry. There really is not much of interest here—except perhaps the Fear mansion."

Her reply startled Daniel. He decided to play innocent. "The Fear mansion? What is so interesting about that?"

Her expression turned serious. She lowered her voice to a whisper. "It is a very frightening place. Horrible stories are told about it. I really do not know if they are true or not. It is said that the Fears live under a terrible curse, that the mansion is cursed, too. It is said that everyone who enters—"

"Every town has a house like that!" Daniel scoffed, shaking his head.

My grandfather's house certainly *looks* like a cursed place, Daniel thought. I wonder why the villagers tell such stories about it.

"I would not venture near it, even for sightseeing," the girl remarked with a frown.

"I will take your advice," Daniel told her. "Would you care to show me around the rest of your town?"

She blushed. A coy smile played over her full lips. "Why, sir, I do not even know your name."

"It is Daniel," he told her eagerly. He started to reveal his full name, but stopped. He realized he didn't want her to know yet that he was a Fear.

"Daniel? I like that name," she replied, her eyes lighting up. "I was once going to name my dog Daniel."

They both laughed.

"And may I ask *your* name?" Daniel asked.

"Nora," she said, pale circles of pink forming on her cheeks. "Nora Goode."

Chapter
25

"Quick—someone's coming!" Nora whispered. She grabbed Daniel's arm and pulled him off the road into the trees.

Daniel laughed. "It's just a rabbit. Look." He pointed to the large brown rabbit that scampered over the carpet of dry leaves at the edge of the woods.

Nora laughed and pressed her forehead against the sleeve of Daniel's jacket.

I love her laugh, he decided.

I love everything about her.

As they walked hand in hand toward the river, Daniel found it hard to believe they had met just five days earlier. He had never felt this way about anyone.

Each afternoon he had waited around the corner from her father's store for her to finish work. Then, trying to make it appear that they weren't walking together, they would make their way up the broad Park Drive to the Conononka River, which flowed through the woods north of the village.

There they would sit side by side and hold hands under a shady tree. As the sun lowered itself behind the cliffs across the river, they talked quietly, getting to know each other, discussing whatever popped into their heads.

Daniel had explained to Nora that he was visiting his grandparents. But he still hadn't worked up the courage to tell her that his grandparents were Simon and Angelica Fear.

"Do your grandparents not wonder where you go every afternoon?" Nora asked. Her dark hair shimmered in the patches of sunlight that filtered down through the tree leaves.

"My grandparents show little desire for my company," Daniel told her. "Most days they do not come out of their rooms. When I do see them, they ask me little. In fact, they hardly speak to me at all."

"How strange," Nora murmured thoughtfully.

"My grandmother lives in a world of her own," Daniel said sadly. "I am not sure she even knows I am her grandson. And my grandfather . . . he spends his days in his wheelchair by the fire, muttering dreamily to himself."

"You must be lonely," Nora remarked, squeezing his hand.

"Not when I see you," Daniel replied boldly.

She smiled at him, her green eyes catching the light of the lowering sun. He realized that Nora must be lonely, too.

Her mother had died in childbirth. Nora was an only child. She spent her days working in her father's general store. She spent her evenings cooking and caring for her father. They lived in rooms above the store.

"My dream is to move away some day," she had revealed to Daniel. "To a town with wide, paved streets and buildings as tall as the trees, a town filled with people I don't know."

As the red sun flattened against the dark cliffs above them, Daniel worked up his nerve, leaned forward, and kissed Nora.

He expected her to resist. But when she returned the kiss with enthusiasm, he realized that perhaps she was as in love with him as he was with her.

I have to reveal to her that I am a Fear, he thought, wrapping his arms around her and kissing her again. But will she react with horror? Does she believe the frightening stories about my family? When she learns I am a Fear, will it drive her away?

The thought made him shudder. Daniel knew he couldn't bear to lose Nora.

As they walked holding hands back to her father's store, Daniel decided he had to learn the truth. Before he revealed his identity to Nora, he had to find out if there really was a curse on his family, if the terrifying tales the villagers told about the Fears were true.

Once I know they are *not* true, once I know they are all silly fairy tales, then I will be able to tell Nora that I am a Fear with a clear heart, he decided.

He said good night at the edge of town, reluctant to let go of her soft, warm hand. Her eyes glowed happily as she whispered good night. Then she turned and ran to the store, her silky dark hair trailing gently behind her.

Her heart fluttering, the taste of Daniel's lips still on hers, Nora brushed through the dark store, humming to herself. Thinking happily about Daniel, she started up the narrow stairs that led to the rooms she shared with her father.

Nora gasped, startled to find her father waiting for her at the top of the stairs, an angry expression on his face.

James Goode, Nora's father, was a short, wiry man with shiny slicked-down black hair and a black pencil mustache beneath his long, pointed nose. He was normally quiet and good-tempered. But when his anger got the better of him, he would explode with rage and lose control so that he frightened Nora.

Now she hesitated halfway up the stairs, staring up at his angry frown, his blazing eyes.

"Where have you been?" he demanded, struggling to keep his voice low and steady.

"Just out for a walk," Nora told him blankly.

He glared at her, his face set in an angry scowl. He motioned for her to come the rest of the way up the stairs. Then he followed her into the small sitting room.

"Just out for a walk with *whom?*" he demanded, crossing his thin arms over the chest of his undershirt.

"With a friend," Nora replied uncomfortably.

"He is no friend," James Goode said through clenched teeth. "The boy you have been sneaking out with is no friend at all—he is a *Fear!*"

Nora gasped. She dropped down onto the straight-backed wooden chair by the fireplace. "He never told me, Father."

"Of course he didn't!" Mr. Goode snapped. "He knew that no decent girl would be seen walking with a Fear in this town!"

"But, Papa—" Nora's mind whirled in confusion. Why hadn't Daniel been honest with her? Was he afraid?

"Papa, Daniel is wonderful," she said finally. "He is kind and gentle. He is intelligent and considerate and—"

"He is a Fear," her father interrupted with a scowl. He stood over Nora, his hands tensed awkwardly at his sides. "I will not have you seeing a Fear. You know the history of that cursed family. Everyone in Shadyside knows."

"I don't *care* about that!" Nora cried. "They are just wild stories."

"Wild stories?" James Goode exclaimed. "Wild stories? Why, Simon Fear's own daughters were *murdered* when they were about your age. Murdered!"

"Papa, that was so long ago!" Nora cried. "No one knows what really happened—"

"The two girls were found in the woods with their bones removed!" James cried. "They found only their skins. Their bones were gone! Gone!"

"You know that's just an old story," Nora screamed. "No one but silly children believes that, Father!"

"Maybe not, but Simon's wife, Angelica, she *is* mad, Nora. She practices evil magic. People have disappeared in the woods behind the Fear mansion. They were Angelica's human sacrifices. They—"

"Papa, stop! These are all wild tales! Gossip and rumors! You *cannot* believe such insane stories!"

James groaned in exasperation, running both hands back through his slicked-down hair, scowling at his daughter. "I *do* believe them," he said, his voice trembling. "I believe them all. This is why I cannot allow you to see that Fear boy again, Nora."

"No!" Nora shrieked, jumping to her feet, her eyes wild. "I *love* Daniel, Father! I *love* him! You *cannot* forbid me to see him!"

"Nora, listen to me," James insisted, his pencil mustache twitching in anger, his slender face reddening. "Listen to me! For your own good, you cannot see him again! I forbid it!"

"No!" Nora shrieked, her anger matching her father's. "No! No! No!"

James Goode's eyes narrowed angrily. His words came out slowly, deliberately, through clenched teeth: "Then, Nora, you have given me no choice. . . ."

Chapter
26

That night Daniel waited until the house was silent and dark. Then, carrying a candle, he crept downstairs to Simon's library, determined to learn the truth about his family's history.

Holding the candle high, Daniel could see that all four walls were covered from floor to ceiling with books. The air smelled musty, almost thick with dust from the old volumes.

The floorboards creaked under Daniel's shoes as he crossed the room to get a closer look at the books. To Daniel's surprise, the first shelf he examined held books about magic, the dark arts, strange scientific journals, and volumes about astrology and foretelling the future.

How strange that Simon should possess books of this nature, Daniel thought, moving the candle along the shelves. Did he and Angelica have a *scientific* interest in such matters?

Daniel searched the library shelves for another twenty minutes but found nothing of interest, nothing that would reveal his family's history to him.

Suddenly hungry and thirsty, he made his way to the kitchen with his candle. The old house creaked and groaned as he walked through the darkness. As if warning me away, he thought, feeling a chill.

A glass of water satisfied his thirst. Then, moving the candle in front of him, Daniel made his way to the pantry behind the kitchen. "Where are those ginger cookies we had at dinner?" he whispered to himself.

He heard the soft scrabble of padded feet. The kitchen cat, no doubt, chasing after a mouse.

He moved the candle over the shelves of tins and jars. No cookies.

Something beyond the pantry shelves caught his attention. A crack in the wall formed a shadow in the flickering candlelight.

Curious, Daniel pressed on the crack, and the wall slid back. *A hidden doorway!* Daniel realized.

His heart beating excitedly, he pushed the door open farther and slipped inside. He found himself in a low-ceilinged narrow room. Holding the candle high, he saw two pillows on the floor, stained by dark mildew, a bundled-up blanket, a girl's doll.

How strange, Daniel thought, bending to pick up the doll. Its dress was covered with dust. Its round blue eyes stared up at him in the candlelight.

Whose doll was this? Daniel wondered, setting it down on one of the pillows. Who used this hidden room? Judging from the dust and mildew, it hasn't been occupied in many years.

He kicked at the blanket, raising a cloud of dust. His shoe hit something solid underneath. "How strange. How strange," he muttered to himself.

He pulled the blanket away and lowered the candle. The light fell over a large dark-covered book. Bending to examine it, Daniel saw that it was an old Bible.

The spine was cracked. The tattered pages smelled of mildew and decay.

This Bible looks as if it has been in the family for many generations, Daniel thought. Why has it been hidden under a blanket in this secret room?

Kneeling on the dusty floor, he began searching through the pages with his free hand. In the back of the Bible he found what he was searching for—a family history.

Tattered, brown-stained pages held the scrawled handwriting of his ancestors. Daniel's eyes eagerly rolled over names and dates, births and deaths.

He saw the date 1692 and read the names Matthew and Benjamin Fier. Wickham, Massachusetts Colony.

Our name was spelled differently then, Daniel realized. I wonder when the change was made—and why.

His eyes eagerly searched the page, reading about other Fiers. So many early deaths, Daniel realized, narrowing his eyes and lowering the candle as he struggled to make out the dates. So many deaths, sometimes two or three at a time.

Bent over the old volume, he turned the page excitedly, his eyes running down the names and dates. Suddenly the candle flickered.

Strange, Daniel thought. There is no breeze in this tiny room.

The candle flickered again.

Had someone else entered the room?

Daniel started to turn as a cold hand was tightly clamped over his mouth.

Chapter
27

Daniel tried to cry out, but the hand gripped tighter.

"Sshhhhh. Do not make a sound," a voice whispered.

The cold hand slipped away. Daniel turned to see Mrs. MacKenzie staring down at him, her glazed-over eye catching the light from his trembling candle. She gave him a strange smile.

"Is it the family history you are looking for?" she whispered, lowering her good eye to the Bible on the floor. "You have no need of books, young master. I will tell you all."

"Wh-what is this room? Why is the family Bible hidden here?" Daniel stammered, climbing unsteadily to his feet.

"I thought it would be safe here," the old housekeeper replied. "This is a secret room. Your aunts, Simon's poor daughters, Hannah and Julia—may they rest in peace—would hide in here to whisper and giggle together. They thought I did not know about this room, but I did."

"How—how did they die?" Daniel demanded.

The old woman raised a finger to her lips. "The curse of the Fears caught up with them."

"Then my family *is* cursed?" Daniel cried. His trembling voice revealed his horror.

"Follow me," Mrs. MacKenzie whispered. "I shall reveal all to you tonight."

He followed her through the dark, twisting halls to her quarters. There, in her tiny, nearly bare room, she motioned with her cane. "Sit you down," the old woman whispered, shoving him toward the high-backed armchair. "I will tell you about the Fears. More than you wish to know."

"The family is really cursed?" Daniel asked again, obediently lowering himself to the chair, staring intently at the old lady in the flickering candlelight. "Are the stories true?"

Mrs. MacKenzie nodded, leaning on her cane. "The curse came about because of your first relatives in the New World. Their names were Matthew and Benjamin Fier."

"I saw those names in the Bible," Daniel told her.

"They were treacherous men. Ambitious. They did not care who they betrayed," the old woman rasped, scowling.

"And the curse? It came about because of them?"

"They burned a young woman at the stake, the Fiers did," Mrs. MacKenzie told him, tapping her cane on the carpet in rhythm with her words. "They burned an *innocent* young woman. Her heartbroken father put a curse on your family.

"From that day on," the old woman continued, "the two families have sought vengeance on each other. Decade after decade, generation after generation, the two families have used all of the evil at their command. They have terrified and betrayed and murdered each other."

She proceeded to tell him the stories of vengeance and betrayal. Daniel listened in chilled silence. Her croaking voice etched the scenes of terror deep into his mind.

"And my grandfather—?" Daniel asked finally, astounded by the old woman's stories.

"Simon Fear thought he could escape the curse by changing the family name. But it followed him. It found him. His young daughters died a horrible death because of it."

The candle trembled in Daniel's hand. He set it down on the arm of the chair.

"Joseph, your father, watched his sister Hannah die. He knew from that moment on that he had to get away from this house, from this village. His brother, Robert, did not get away. He died of a strange fever, many said brought on by a spell from his evil daughter-in-law, Sarah Fear. The other brother, Brandon, and his son Ben—they just wandered into the woods and disappeared. The curse . . .

"The curse of the two families continues to this day," the old woman said, shaking her head.

"The other family," Daniel whispered. "What is their name?"

Mrs. MacKenzie hesitated. She coughed, leaning on her cane.

"Mrs. MacKenzie, please tell me," Daniel urged. "What is the name of the other family, the family that has cursed mine?"

"Their name is Goode," the old woman revealed.

Daniel gasped. "Goode? But that cannot be!" he sputtered. "Mrs. MacKenzie, I—I am in love with a Goode! Nora Goode! She cannot possibly be related to the evil family who—"

"She is a Goode," the housekeeper replied solemnly, staring hard at Daniel, leaning into the candlelight.

"No!" Daniel cried, leaping to his feet. "No! I cannot accept this! Nora is kind and gentle. She is innocent of any evil. I am certain she knows nothing of this curse!"

"Perhaps she does not know," Mrs. MacKenzie replied, leaning on the cane. "Perhaps you and she will be the ones to break the curse."

"Break the curse?" Daniel asked eagerly. He grabbed the old woman, "Break the curse? How?"

"If a Fear and a Goode were to marry . . ." Mrs. MacKenzie said thoughtfully.

"Yes!" Daniel cried, his voice cutting through the heavy, musty air. "Yes! Thank you, Mrs. MacKenzie! That is what I shall do! And the curse will end forever!"

* * *

The next morning passed so slowly, Daniel felt as if time were standing still. Pacing his room, he repeatedly checked his pocket watch, waiting for the time when Nora finished work.

Downstairs, preparations for Simon's birthday party were under way. The party was scheduled for that evening. Simon and Angelica had not emerged from their rooms. But a line of carts and carriages pulled up to the back entrance, carrying food and drink and flowers for the celebration.

At a little after three Daniel set off, walking toward town. It was a lengthy walk along a dirt path that led through woods, fields, then finally small houses before reaching the town square. But Daniel enjoyed the walk. It gave him a chance to think of Nora and to rehearse what he planned to say to her.

It was a warm day for autumn, almost summer-like. Daniel unbuttoned his heavy overcoat as he walked. After several minutes more he removed it and slung it over a shoulder.

When the low brick buildings of the town square came into view, Daniel's heart began to pound. He had rehearsed his marriage proposal again and again, repeating the words in his mind.

But what, he wondered, would Nora's reaction be?

Daniel knew that Nora liked him and cared about him. But what would happen when he revealed to her that he was a Fear? What would happen when he told her the long tragic history of their families? When he told her that their marriage would end a centuries-old curse on their families?

Would she be horrified—or overjoyed?

Taking a deep breath, he shifted the coat to his other shoulder and crossed the unpaved street, taking long strides.

The white clapboard general store came into view. Daniel felt as if his heart would burst!

He stepped onto the sidewalk—and stopped short.

The store window was boarded over with pine boards.

The door, normally open, was shut. Behind the small window in the door, the store was dark as night. And empty.

Nora is gone, Daniel realized.

Chapter
28

Daniel staggered back, nearly toppling over. "Where is she?" he cried, staring in horror at the boarded-up store. "Where has she gone?"

He stood, trying to make sense of his frantic, rambling thoughts, trying to decide what to do next.

How could she disappear overnight? Vanish into thin air?

As he stood in shock and dismay, a voice floated toward him, calling him, "Daniel! Daniel!" *Nora's voice!*

He uttered a low cry of surprise, then held his breath, listening hard.

Again he heard her voice. Again he heard her calling his name from far away, so far away. So faint and far away that it could be the wind. Or his imagination.

"Daniel! Daniel!"

"Nora, I hear you!" he cried frantically. "Where are you? Where?"

He listened again. It *is* my imagination, he decided miserably.

His shoulders slumped forward. The sky darkened. He felt like collapsing into the dirt.

"Daniel! Daniel!"

The faint, faraway cries were going to drive him mad.

"Daniel! Daniel!"

Desperately Nora called to him, pounding on the frame of her bedroom window above the store until her fists throbbed with pain.

"Look up! Why won't you look up?" she pleaded, watching Daniel, his face darkened by shock and grief.

"Daniel! Daniel! Up here!" she screamed.

Finally he glanced up. Finally he saw her. "Nora!" She could hear his happy cry through the glass.

Wiping away her tears, she pointed frantically to the narrow balcony outside her second-floor window. It took him only a few seconds to realize she wanted him to climb the drainpipe to the balcony.

She watched as he tossed his heavy coat to the ground, grabbed the pipe with both hands, and began to pull himself up.

Behind him, she saw, the village square stood empty, except for a large yellow hound dog sleeping in the middle of the street. "Hurry! Please hurry!" Nora begged, her hands pressed against the thick windowpane.

A short while later he was standing outside her window, breathing hard. He stared in at her tearstained face. "Nora, what has happened?" he demanded. "Open the window!"

"I cannot!" she called out to him. "My father has locked it! I am locked in my room!"

She watched him grip the frame and struggle to pry the window up. It wouldn't budge.

With a loud groan he pressed his shoulder against the glass and leaned with all his weight. The pane remained in place.

Nora leapt back as Daniel heaved his shoulder into the pane again. She cried out as the glass fell into her room. It landed flat at her feet without shattering.

With a happy cry Daniel burst through the popening and swept Nora into his arms.

"Daniel! Daniel, I thought I would never see you again!" Nora cried, pressing her damp cheek against his.

He hugged her tight. "Nora, what has happened? Why has your father locked you in here?"

She held on to him for a moment, as if proving to herself that he was solid, that he was real. "Father locked me in to make sure I would never see you again. He has gone to the next town to make arrangements. He is taking us far away, Daniel. Far away."

Daniel uttered a cry of surprise. "But why, Nora?"

"He found out that you are a Fear," Nora replied, her body trembling, tears rolling down her flushed cheeks.

"So you know!" Daniel said, feeling his pulse throb at his temples. "You know I am a member of that cursed family!"

"I know, and I do not care!" Nora declared. "I love you, Daniel! I do not care anything about your family or its past!"

"I love you, too, Nora!" Daniel cried, and they embraced again. "But you must know the story of our families. You must know all about the curse."

"No! Take me away from here!" Nora pleaded, her voice trembling. "For Father will never allow us to be together. He will be back in an hour or two. And then—"

"That is time enough for me to tell the story," Daniel insisted. "And then we will be married!"

"Yes!" Nora agreed, squeezing his hand. "Oh, yes, Daniel!" They kissed.

Holding her hands tightly, Daniel revealed to Nora the tragic history of the Fears and the Goodes. She listened in horrified silence, leaning her head against his shoulder.

"So many deaths, so much murder and betrayal," she murmured when Daniel had finished.

"Does this mean that you will not marry me?" he asked, his eyes burning into hers.

"We must be married at once," she replied breathlessly. "We must end the curse forever."

Daniel cried out in happiness. "I passed by the house of the town justice on my way here. I know he will marry us now!"

Nora's smile faded. She gazed at him uncertainly. "But, Daniel, we have no ring to bind the ceremony."

Daniel let go of her hand. His expression turned thoughtful. "No ring . . ." he muttered, frowning. "Oh. Wait!" He reached behind his neck and pulled off the silver three-clawed pendant. "This will serve as a ring, Nora!" he proclaimed excitedly.

"What a strange object!" Nora cried, staring at it. "Where did you get it?"

"It is of no concern," Daniel replied excitedly. "It will serve as a ring." He raised the silver disk to slip the chain around her neck.

As she arranged the pendant, Nora felt a sudden surge of heat at her chest and thought she saw flames rising up around the room. The strange image lasted only a few seconds. When it cleared, Daniel was pulling her by the hand toward the window to make their escape.

"Tonight is my grandfather Simon's seventy-fifth birthday party," Daniel told her, helping her onto the tiny balcony outside the window. "We will announce our marriage at the party!"

"Oh, Daniel!" Nora cried, lingering at the window. "What will your grandfather say? What if our announcement angers him or makes him un-happy?"

"He can only be joyful that a centuries-old curse has ended," Daniel replied, smiling, his dark eyes flashing excitedly. "Come, Nora. Hurry! Tonight will be a night we will long remember!"

Chapter
29

===============

T hat night Daniel walked with his new
bride through the gloomy halls of his grandfather's
mansion.

"Daniel, this house . . . it frightens me," Nora
whispered.

"We shall not stay long, dear wife," Daniel told
her, squeezing her hand. "We will leave after the
birthday party. I promise. We will not even stay the
night."

Nora stayed close by his side as he led her
through the dark corridors of Simon Fear's house.
"The house is so dark, so cold," she whispered.

"Try not to think gloomy thoughts," he urged as
the pantry came into view. "After all, we are
married. And after a few hours we never need
return to this dreary place again."

Mrs. MacKenzie and more than a dozen helpers, hired from another town for the evening, were bustling about the kitchen, preparing the food and drink for the birthday party. But the old housekeeper stopped to stare as Daniel led Nora into the room.

"Mrs. MacKenzie, this is my wife, Nora," Daniel announced, unable to keep a wide, excited grin from his face.

"Nora Goode," the old woman muttered, studying Nora intently with her one good eye. Then she smiled, too. "I wish you both joy," she said.

"Please take care of Nora while I attend to my grandparents," Daniel asked, still holding his bride's hand. "When the time is right, I plan to announce our marriage."

He turned before the housekeeper could react and hurried to greet Simon and Angelica in the ballroom.

Daniel stopped in surprise at one entrance to the ballroom.

Where are the guests? he asked himself.

The enormous room was empty. Hundreds of glimmering candles sent a wash of pale light over the walls, festooned with white and yellow flowers.

Daniel's footsteps echoed loudly in the vast emptiness as he crossed the room to greet his grandparents.

The party was scheduled to have begun more than an hour ago, he remembered. Was it possible that no one had come?

As far as Daniel had been able to tell during the weeks of his visit, his grandparents had no friends. The Fear mansion had been closed to all visitors for thirty-five years.

Did Simon and Angelica expect people to come? Had they invited anyone? Anyone besides Daniel?

Daniel felt a chill of horror.

Am I really the only guest at this eerie party?

"Hello!" he called, trying to sound cheerful. But his voice echoed mournfully in the enormous empty space.

His grandparents hovered near the door.

Angelica wore a solemn-looking black dress more suited to a funeral than a birthday party. Her long white hair was tied behind her head with a black ribbon.

Daniel hesitated and gaped at his grandmother.

Angelica was going through the motions of welcoming guests. "So good to see you," she repeated with a smile, nodding her head at empty air. "So nice of you to come."

Daniel swallowed hard. She has entirely lost her senses! he told himself, watching her smiling and carrying on a conversation with no one at all.

Simon, his dark eyes glowing excitedly behind his spectacles, his face flushed in the candlelight, stared eagerly at the open doorway. He leaned forward in his wheelchair, an expectant smile frozen on his face, as if eager to see who would arrive next.

Daniel took a deep breath. I guess I had better go along with the charade, he told himself with a shudder. "Happy birthday, Grandfather," he called warmly, rushing up to the wheelchair and shaking Simon's hand.

Simon's hand was as cold as ice. "Thank you, my boy," he replied. "I am happy that at least *one* member of my family saw fit to attend this occasion," he added with some bitterness.

Daniel moved over to greet Angelica. "Did you come with the Bridgers?" she asked. She stared at him as if she had never seen him before.

"You . . . uh . . . look lovely tonight, Grandmother," Daniel managed to say.

"Don't just stand there. Why don't you mingle with our guests?" Angelica demanded. She turned away from him and stuck out her gloved hand. "So good of you to come," she gushed to no one at all. "And how are your lovely daughters?"

Simon continued to stare at the doorway, the expectant smile frozen on his face.

Daniel stepped quickly to the wall, his shoes pounding like thunder in the empty ballroom.

What should I do? he wondered. They are mad, completely mad—both of them!

Should I bring Nora out and introduce her now? Shall I tell them that Nora and I have married?

Or should I take Nora and flee this frightening place?

No. I cannot run. I must stay and tell them.

Watching Simon from across the room, Daniel wondered how the old man would react. A Fear had married a Goode. Today, on Simon's birthday, the ancient feud between the two families had ended.

Hundreds of years of bitterness, of treachery, of evil, had come to an end. The Fears and the Goodes would be one family now.

Will my grandfather share my joy? Daniel wondered.

Daniel heard a rumbling from the far end of the ballroom. He glanced up to see a birthday cake being wheeled in on a cart.

It was an enormous round cake, three tall tiers, frosted in white and yellow. On top were seventy-five candles, creating a blaze of yellow light that shimmered over the cake.

This is absurd! Daniel thought. Such a magnificent cake for such an empty celebration.

Who would bring such a cake into a tomb! A *tomb!*

I've got to get Nora now, he decided. I will tell my grandparents my news. And then Nora and I will flee into the night, never to return!

As the hired servants slowly wheeled the cake toward Simon and Angelica, Daniel hurried to the pantry to retrieve Nora. Holding her hand tightly, he pulled her into the ballroom.

In the gloomy, eerie silence, Simon was preparing to blow out the candles, his face red in the glow from seventy-five candles.

Nora resisted, but Daniel pulled her across the empty ballroom. Squeezing her hand, he gave her a reassuring smile. She looks so beautiful, Daniel thought.

Nora wore a simple pale blue dress with a lacy

white collar. The silver three-toed pendant glowed at her throat.

"Grandfather, Grandmother, I have an announcement to make," Daniel declared, his voice booming in the empty room. Nora lingered just behind him.

Daniel saw Simon's eyes narrow. Simon was staring at the pendant at Nora's throat. "Wh—what is this?" he stammered.

Holding tightly to Nora's hand, Daniel took a deep breath. "Grandfather, on this happy occasion I—I would like to introduce my wife to you. I have married Nora Goode!"

Chapter
30

"*N*ooooooo!"

A hideous wail, a cry of anguish and of horror rose over the ballroom, causing a thousand candles to flicker and bend low.

It took Nora a long while to realize that the howl had come from Simon Fear.

Frightened, she took a few steps back as Simon rose from his wheelchair. The old man's eyes were wide with horror. He pointed a trembling finger at the three-clawed disk around Nora's throat.

"*Nooooooo!*" Another animal howl escaped Simon's lips.

Still pointing, he staggered toward her.

But his legs would not support him. He stumbled. Trying to steady himself, he leaned against the cart and pushed over the cake.

Angelica began to shriek as the enormous cake splattered to the floor.

"Daniel, what shall we do?" Nora cried. But her words were drowned out by yet another howl from Simon and by Angelica's shrill cries.

"Daniel, what is happening?"

A small carpet caught fire first. Then the entire room was ablaze—as if all the candles in the ballroom had suddenly fallen and flared into tall flames.

"Daniel, please! Daniel!"

She couldn't see him. He was hidden behind a bright wall of fire only feet from her.

Flames leapt from the floor and danced off the four walls.

How could the room be burning so quickly? Nora wondered, choking on the thick smoke, choking on her fear. "Daniel? Daniel?"

It was so bright, so blindingly bright.

As she stared into the flames, surrounded by screams and terrified cries, Nora saw a struggling figure emerge from the yellow-orange brightness.

"Daniel? Where *are* you?"

The figure grew closer, clearer.

Nora raised her hand to her mouth as she realized she was staring at a girl about her age, a girl struggling against a dark wooden stake, surrounded by flames, a girl burning, burning, burning, screaming as she burned. Susannah Goode, burning at the stake beside her mother.

And as Nora gaped in open-mouthed horror,

other tortured figures invaded the room, rising up through the crackling, blistering flames.

Nora saw Rebecca Fier, her neck broken, hanging by a rope from a dark rafter. Old Benjamin Fier rose into the room, impaled like a scarecrow, a wooden shaft pushed up through the back of his skull.

Nora screamed and tried to shut her eyes. But she had to watch, she had to bear witness as the other victims of the past emerged in the burning ballroom.

As she stared in silent horror, she saw Matthew and Constance Fier, skeletons behind their walled-up prison. William Goode, his head exploded, his skull showing through rotted flesh, hovered into view.

The ghost of little Abigail Goode floated overhead. Abigail's mother, Jane, staggered stiffly after her, her face bloated from drowning. Kate Fier rose in front of them, a knitting needle through her heart. Hannah Fear came next, a sword through her chest.

Then Nora saw Julia Fear, scratching the air, scratching at nothing, her fingernails cut and bleeding. Poor Julia, buried alive, but back now to join the other victims of the centuries.

The victims, the phantoms of the past, Fears and Goodes, roared around the room, their cries louder than the thunder of the flames. They swept round and round, faster, faster, until they became a raging whirlwind of pain, of brutal death.

"Daniel, where are you? Daniel?"

Nora stared into the swirling flame. "Daniel, oh, Daniel!"

Unable to find him, unable to endure the howls of the dead, their cries of agony as they swept around the room, Nora covered her eyes and fled.

Moments later she was in the cool darkness of the night, watching the blaze from the front lawn, trembling from the sudden cold, gripping the silver medallion with both hands as villagers made their way from town and gathered, muttering about the evil of the Fears, about the centuries of evil that had led to this night, to this final fire.

"Daniel! Please come out, Daniel!"

Nora called his name again and again.

But as the flames raged, swallowing the Fear mansion in their eerie light, and the terrifying howls rose up in the night like a symphony of pain and horror, Nora knew she would never see Daniel again.

Epilogue

N̲ora dipped her pen, but the inkwell had run dry. Yawning, she set down the pen and stared at the stack of pages she had written.

Our marriage ended the feud between the Fears and the Goodes, she thought miserably. But not as we had intended.

No one came out of the fire. Not Daniel. No one.

The house burned for days until the fire finally smoldered out, leaving nothing but a black, charred shell in its place. Leaving the charred ruins of the Fear mansion and a legacy of evil—evil that will hover over the entire village.

This is why I have written my story, Nora thought, flexing her aching fingers. This is why I have spent the night writing down everything I know about the Goodes and the Fears.

Maybe someone reading this will be able to stop the evil before it rises again.

They think I am insane, Nora realized. They think the fire and all I saw drove me mad.

That is why they brought me to this insane asylum. That is why they locked me in this room.

But I am not mad. My story had to be told. It had to be written. I had to stop the hideous evil. I *had* to.

Glancing at the sunlight pouring through the window, Nora heard footsteps. Voices in the hall.

The door to her room opened. Two uniformed nurses entered. Their faces were solemn, their eyes cold. "The doctors will see you now, Nora," one of them said softly.

"Yes. Very well," Nora said, rising from the hard chair she had spent the night in. She lifted the heavy sheaf of papers from the small desk. "Here. They must read this," she told the nurse. "They must read the whole story. They must know about the evil. The evil will destroy us all, you see. They must know—"

Narrowing her eyes, studying Nora's face, the nurse took Nora's pages and tossed them into the fire.

"No!" Nora shrieked. She tried to dive after them, but the nurses held her back firmly.

"It is for your own good, Nora," one of them said softly. "If the doctors saw what you have spent the night scribbling, they would lock you up and throw away the key."

Nora stared at her pages as they caught flame and started to burn, sending thick white smoke up the chimney.

"You do not understand!" she protested, tears forming in her tired eyes. "The evil is still alive. The evil is still there! The word must get out. People must know—"

"Come with us, Nora." The nurse's voice was soft, but her grip was hard and tight on Nora's arm. "Come with us now. Try to forget your wild tale."

"Did you not hear the news?" the other nurse asked brightly. "This will surely cheer you, Nora. The Fear mansion is gone, but the village is to build a road on the property."

"What? A road?" Nora asked, feeling dazed. "But the horror—"

"No more horror, Nora. No more. The road will be lovely. It means that lovely houses will be built there," the nurse told her, edging her toward the door. "And do you know what they're going to call the new road?"

"What?" Nora asked weakly.

"They're going to call it Fear Street."

About the Author

"Where do you get your ideas?"

That's the question that R.L. Stine is asked most often. "I don't know where my ideas come from," he says. "But I do know that I have a lot more scary stories in my mind that I can't wait to write."

So far, R.L. has written more than one hundred mysteries and thrillers for young people, all of them bestsellers.

R.L. grew up in Columbus, Ohio. Today he lives in an apartment near Central Park in New York City with his wife, Jane.

THE NIGHTMARES
NEVER END . . .
WHEN YOU VISIT

Next . . .
SILENT NIGHT II

Wealthy, spoiled Reva Dalby is back—and Pres Nichols is out to get her. Pres and his friend Diane are broke, but Pres knows how they can get a million dollars . . . just in time for Christmas.

Pres and Diane decide to kidnap Reva and demand a million dollars ransom.

Can they do it? Can they get away with it? Will Reva get out of this alive?

DARK SECRETS™
by Elizabeth Chandler

Who is Megan? She's about to find out....

#1: Legacy of Lies

Megan thought she knew who she was.

Until she came to Grandmother's house.

Until she met Matt, who angered and attracted her as no boy ever had before.

Then she began having dreams again, of a life she never lived, a love she never

knew...a secret that threatened to drive her to the grave.

❖

Home is where the horror is....

#2: Don't Tell

Lauren is coming home, eight years after her mother's mysterious drowning. They said

it was an accident. But the tabloids screamed murder. Aunt Jule was her only refuge,

the beloved second mother she's returning to see. But first Lauren stops at Wisteria's

annual street festival and meets Nick, a tease, a flirt, and a childhood playmate.

The day is almost perfect—until she realizes she's being watched.

A series of nasty "accidents" makes Lauren realize someone wants her dead.

And this time there's no place to run....

❖

Published by Simon & Schuster

FEAR STREET

R·L·STINE

GOODNIGHT KISS
◆Collector's Edition◆

Includes

Goodnight Kiss
Their first kiss could be her last....

Goodnight Kiss 2
It's the kiss of death.

Plus...

The Vampire Club
A NEW Vampire story by R.L. Stine

Published by Simon & Schuster

1360-02